The door flew open, and he was confronted by a small woman with alarm-filled eyes.

She was drenched from head to toe.

The instant she saw him, her expression of waterlogged alarm brightened. Before Nate had time to react, she latched on to him and all but yanked him across the threshold.

Like Old Faithful, water spewed out from behind the washing machine. Soaked within moments, Nate saw the ancient, brittle water valve had broken, causing the gusher.

He'd expected to come over, make his welcome known and head out. But he couldn't leave her stranded like this. "I'm Nate Talbert. Your neighbor," he offered.

"It's nice to meet you," she said. "I'm Pollyanna McDonald."

Nate wasn't sure how to react. Frankly, he wasn't too keen on the idea of a neighbor who didn't even know how to get out of the rain, so to speak. It didn't bode well. Not at all.

Next Door Daddy
Debra Clopton

Steeple
Hill®

Published by Steeple Hill Books™

STEEPLE HILL BOOKS

Steeple
Hill®

ISBN-13: 978-0-373-87464-4
ISBN-10:   0-373-87464-2

NEXT DOOR DADDY

Copyright © 2008 by Debra Clopton

www.SteepleHill.com

Printed in U.S.A.

The Lord is my strength and my song;
he has become my salvation.
—*Psalms* 118:14

To Wayne: your love, your laughter
and your strength live on.

Acknowledgments

First I want to thank God for giving me this purpose.
He is truly amazing.

I also want to thank my editor, Krista Stroever,
who has shared a love and vision for my
Mule Hollow series from the very beginning.
Her hard work and excellent eye for cutting
to the heart of the book has been a blessing.

I want to thank Emily Rodmell, who assisted with
many duties during some of my past books and
Elizabeth Mazer, who is assisting my editor now,
you are wonderful. Thank you both for all you do.

Thank you to the entire wonderful team working
with me at Steeple Hill and Harlequin Books.

And thank you, Joyce Hart, my agent, who took
one look at my first book set in Mule Hollow and
believed in me.

Chapter One

You are not a plumber, Pollyanna McDonald reminded herself as she eyed the thin trail of water trickling from beneath the bolt…or was it called a socket?

A lug nut?

Whatever—she might not be able to put a finger on the name of the doohickey, thing, but her washing machine was connected to it and she didn't have to know its name in order to fix it.

Surely she could take care of that little, tiny water leak. They did it on HGTV all the time. Piece of cake. Women of all ages, shapes, sizes and ethnicities fixed any manner of things on those shows all the time and so could she.

Lifting her chin, she hiked the tool belt into a more comfortable position on her hips and hoped for confidence. The assortment of sparkling tools tinkled like wind chimes in the pockets, drawing her to study them. What in the world did one *do* with this many wrenches? They all looked the same.

Obviously Marc had found uses for all of them; they'd come from his toolbox, after all. She reached for one. *You are not a plumber—*

"Yet," she said out loud, firmly silencing the negative voice in her head. She'd been pushing herself for two years to do and be more than she'd ever thought she could be. She could tighten a silly piece of metal.

Shhh-whump! Whump! The resounding thud and immediate echo from the front room of the house sent Polly's heart skittering to a halt.

The exuberant "Ye-haw!" jump-started it up again. Followed by two small feet charging her way.

That banister was going to be the death of her. It was. And she'd have no one to blame but herself when she dropped in her tracks.

Any woman in her right mind should have known an eight-year-old-boy with daredevil genes would take one look at the gorgeous, three-story, gracefully winding stair railing and see the ultimate joyride.

"That's one *doozy* of a ride, Mom!" her son, Gilly, howled. Fresh cheeks glowing, eyes twinkling with the elation of living life full tilt he burst into the room, racing by on his way to the back door.

Despite the wave of anxiety that overcame her every time he shot down the banister, his enthusiasm made Polly smile when she needed to censure.

Toenails churning as he sought traction on the hardwood, Bogie, Gilly's seven-month-old puppy, could be heard making his way through the house in hot pursuit. The wrinkled shar-pei was smile material, too, in his oversize birthday suit. His already comical appearance was made more so since, for medical reasons and not vanity, he'd had to have "some work" done on his droopy eyelids. Because of this he was wearing a hard plastic collar that resembled a lampshade and prevented him from scratching out the stitches. It was also dangerous to his health as it messed up his depth perception. Polly feared the worst as she watched the doorway for him to make his entrance. As expected, he misjudged the turn, snagged the contraption on the door frame and was sent sprawling to the floor. Poor Pepper, their cockatiel, aka dog jockey, as he loved to perch on Bogie's back, was ejected at impact and sent flying into the air!

Never a dull moment. Polly wasn't sure who was more embarrassed, the dog or the bird, as Pepper made a drunken becline for the open cabinet door beside where Polly stood and glared at Bogie.

"Busted!" Pepper squealed in his childlike voice. "*Buu*-sted."

Thanks to Marc, Pepper had a huge vocabulary. Because of her husband's tutelage, a person could practically hold a conversation with the spunky fowl.

Watching the bedlam, Gil cringed. Polly saw his eyes melt with sympathy and her heart swelled with love for her son. *Thank you, Lord.*

"Poor Bogie. C'mon, little buddy," he said, bending forward and patting his knee. Poor Bogie needed all the encouragement he could get. Curly tail flattened out and hanging low, he trudged over, looking like Eeyore, and sat on Gil's feet, his face averted from view.

"It's okay, little fella," Gil cooed, affectionately rubbing Bogie's ears. He had itchy ears and loved a good rub. And Polly loved that her son had inherited his father's way with animals. Watching his gentleness never ceased to touch her. She could almost feel Marc smiling beside her.

Swallowing the lump in her throat, she crooked her elbows, setting her fist on her hips, just above that monster of a tool belt.

"I'll call you when dinner's ready. But don't go too far."

"I won't," Gil called, pushing open the door, allowing Bogie plenty of room to make it out without further mishap. "You stay here, Pepper," Gil instructed unnecessarily.

Pepper bobbed and weaved from his perch but didn't try to follow. "Chicken! Chicken!" he chanted instead.

Gil laughed and glanced back at Polly. "Hey, you fixin' to work on something?" he asked, taking in the tool belt for the first time.

"Just a little water leak. You go ahead and play. This won't take long."

"Aw, Mom, you sure? Maybe I could help. I *am* the man of the house now."

Polly's heart hit a speed bump. "I know, dear. But this won't take a second. I'll let you help me next time."

He looked as if he wanted to say more, then shrugged and headed out to play. Polly felt guilty about not letting him help, but she needed to learn how to do things for herself before she could teach him.

Pepper flew from the cabinet door to perch on the curtain rod at the window, the perfect place to watch Gil and Bogie play on the lawn.

Polly crossed to the window. A semblance of contentment settled over her as she watched Gil and Bogie frolic on the hillside. Her heart tightened…she'd done it. She'd actually moved her son from the city. He was going to grow up in the country with room to run and raise all kinds of animals…just like his daddy had wanted him to.

And she'd chosen well. She felt it in her heart. From the moment she and Gil and their menagerie had pulled into the small Texas town of Mule Hollow four days ago they'd been embraced by the locals. She was expecting many of them back tomorrow to help with the daunting task of setting up her kitchen.

For a woman who desperately needed a new start and had just taken a huge leap of faith by moving here, the town's warm welcome was a much-needed and appreciated assurance that God was looking after her and her son.

They'd come a long way in more ways than one in the two years since Marc's death. But with the Lord's help they were making it. Marc would be proud of the way they'd learned…were *learning* to be independent.

With renewed determination, she turned from the window and eyed the leak that was slowly soaking the pile of towels. Looking down, she pulled a wrench from one of the pockets of Marc's tool belt then looked up at Pepper. "What do you think, Pep? Time to rock 'n' roll?"

"Rock 'n' roll! *Rooock* 'n' roll!" Pepper quipped, and immediately busted into his signature duck-and-dive dance down the length of the curtain rod. Something else Marc had taught him.

Polly chuckled, took a deep breath and squeezed behind the washing machine. If that bird could learn to talk and dance, *she,* Pollyanna McDonald, could learn to fix a water leak.

Reba crooned a ballad on the radio as Nate Talbert, arm crooked out the open window, drove his Dodge up the gravel drive toward home. His attention was snagged by movement on the hill across the pasture. The kid and his odd-looking dog were wrestling on the front lawn of the recently inhabited house. Since the house had been vacant for years, the idea of having neighbors still hadn't sunk in totally for Nate. It was going to take some getting used to.

He'd been secluded out here; it suited him. Especially for the past three years.

As dust trailed behind him, Nate watched the dog run in wild awkward circles around the kid. The pup was wearing a protective collar, so it must have had some sort of work done. When the stiff plastic snagged in the grass it did a number on the pup, flipping him like a flapjack, straight over onto his back. The kid tumbled to the ground beside him, laughing and rubbing the dog's exposed belly. Despite himself, Nate smiled as he drove around the bend toward his home.

He was still thinking about the carefree picture the kid and the dog made as he exited his truck and strode toward the barn. He knew the neighborly thing to do was to go over and introduce himself. Everybody else in town already had…but he wasn't neighborly. He would have preferred it if the house had remained empty. He wasn't sociable and he certainly wasn't looking to trade cups of sugar with anyone.

They'd know this about him soon enough, so what did it matter. The very idea of someone being near enough to interrupt his solitude was unsettling.

"Hey, Taco, how's my bud?" he asked the large bay who stuck his head out of the stall. Instantly, Taco snorted and kicked his big head back and forth, his signal that he was ready for a run. Nate agreed, and within moments he had the horse saddled and loping across the barnyard toward open pasture. He had plenty of work to keep him busy, but some days, just like Taco, Nate needed to feel the sun on his face and the wind rushing across his skin as he sought a semblance of peace.

The sight of the kid and the dog romping in their yard tugged at him as he rode. He'd wanted children. He and Kayla had dreamed of a large family. The bitter sense of dreams lost surged to the forefront of his memory like the bite of a bucket of ice water tossed at him.

Just as ruthlessly, he shoved the thoughts back into the dark corners of his mind.

It was easier that way. Still, the kid and the dog refused to disappear from his thoughts. They were his new neighbors. They'd lived next door to him for almost a week and he'd yet to show *any* kind of Texas hospitality. Forget Texas hospitality; he hadn't shown any kind of hospitality. His Kayla would have nailed his hide to the barn for his bad behavior, and he didn't even want to think about what his mother would do if she got wind of it. Not that he'd worried too much about etiquette since he'd laid Kayla to rest three years ago.

During that time the entire town had given him a wide berth, but lately they'd begun to try to ease him back into the fold. He'd given in on occasion, almost as if willing a change to happen inside of him. It hadn't.

He'd heard in town at the feed store that the kid's mother was a widow woman. That knowledge alone should make him ashamed of his neglect. He knew the hardships that came with losing a wife. A widow with a kid would have even more struggles to overcome and deal with… His conscience pricked, hitting a nerve.

The saddle creaked as he shifted in the seat and glanced back over his shoulder to the house that had come into view. He should just drop by, introduce himself.

Welcome the woman and her son. Meet the dog.

But it wouldn't end there. His grip tightened uncertainly. Propriety would demand that he offer to help her out with anything she might have a problem with. That was where the hesitancy came in. He'd been operating on autopilot for so long, dug in so deep into himself, that even the idea of opening a window for someone was a struggle. And there was the other issue to think of…

He lived in a town that had gone crazy over matching folks up and marrying them off. The last thing he wanted was to get any kind of expectation started about him and some woman. A widow woman at that.

Nope, that was a place he wasn't willing to go. Turning away he started to head back home.

But Kayla would have wanted him to show his manners. It went without saying that the Lord would, too.

Taco drew up of his own accord, and before he could back out of the idea he turned Taco west and loped down the hill toward the house. He might as well get it out of the way or he wasn't going to have any peace.

Leaving Taco tied to the fence, he ducked between the middle strands of barbed wire and strode across the yard. The kid and the dog were nowhere in sight as he headed toward the back porch. It was closer, and he didn't see any reason to waste time tramping to the front of the house…besides the fact that he was in his dusty work clothes. As he stepped up onto the small porch, he could hear muffled sounds on the other side of the heavy wooden door. He paused, lifting his hand to knock as the strange sounds radiated through the door.

Shoving his hat back, he put an ear close to the doorjamb. *What in the world?* A high-pitched childlike voice was screaming something he couldn't make out on the other side. Nate's pulse spiked as he slammed his knuckles against the door. "Hey," he shouted, pounding.

Almost instantly, before he could get another shout out the door flew open and he was confronted by a small woman with alarm-filled eyes. She was drenched from head to toe and wearing a tool belt stuffed with what appeared to be every possible tool known to man. It had to weigh more than she did.

The instant she saw him her expression of water-logged alarm brightened. "Oh, hallelujah!" she exclaimed. "You are the answer to my prayers!"

Before Nate had time to react she latched on to him and all but yanked him across the threshold.

Chapter Two

It was pandemonium! Nate registered as he was half dragged across the threshold.

"I'm melting! I'm melting!"

The screaming now became clear and continued frantically from somewhere. Not exactly the words he was expecting, but confusing nonetheless as he scanned the chaos going on around him.

Like Old Faithful, water hissed and spewed up and out from behind the washing machine while the eerie screaming rolled on over and over. "I'm *mel*-ting! I'm *melll*-ting!"

Standing directly in the path of the gusher was the boy, seeming to be having the time of his life. At his knees, the dog that had been romping and playing earlier now hunkered down behind him.

"Hi-ya, mister!" The kid laughed.

Adrenaline pumping, Nate barely took time to nod as he searched for the screamer. His attention was drawn upward, where of all things, a small green bird perched on the top of the curtain rod. It was chanting and screeching its weird little head off as it fluffed its wings out, catching the light spray of water barely reaching it across the room.

Like the kid, the bird was having the time of its life.

"Can you help me?" the woman asked, blinking through the water.

Soaked within moments of entering the room, Nate saw at a glance that the ancient water valve had broken, causing the unforgiving gusher.

The dog howled mournfully as if to say "Please do something." The kid spun. The bird sang.

Nate raked his hand down his dripping face and looked around the room. "Where's your shutoff valve?" he called over the ruckus.

The woman gulped hard, the panic in her eyes free-falling into despair. "I don't *know*. I didn't think to ask."

Just what he needed, a crying woman—not that he'd see the tears for all the water. He exited the house in search of the outside shutoff valve. Sadly, everyone followed him.

Except the bird, who could still be heard happily melting in the background.

"Where ya going, mister?" the kid huffed, jogging to match Nate's long stride. His arms pumped back and forth, slinging water in all directions.

"The pump house," Nate grunted. He could hear the woman behind him clinking and clacking with every step.

"What for?" the kid asked.

"It'll have a shutoff valve," Nate said, reaching the squat building. Wasting no time he yanked open the door and stepped inside. The kid and the grunting dog followed him into the tiny space. He heard the dog's plastic collar scrape the door frame behind him, followed by a grunt and a thud.

"So that's a shutoff, huh?" the boy said, peering around Nate as clasped the red handle and yanked down.

"Yup," he muttered. Through the dim light the boy looked up at him, his expression solemn.

"I'm the man of the house. I need to know these things."

The earnest way he stated this fact twisted Nate's gut. This boy, no more than eight or nine, had lost his dad and was trying to step up to the plate. His sincerity tugged at even Nate's numb, unresponsive heart. "That's the main shutoff," he explained brusquely, easing around the kid and out the door. He was out of his element here.

The woman was waiting, and to his great relief she wasn't falling apart anymore. "Thank you," she said, fully composed, her big green eyes clear. "I'm so sorry you had to get soaked, but it just broke in my hand and I couldn't— I didn't know what to do. I panicked."

He heard the disgust in her voice and he wasn't sure if it was from the valve breaking or that she'd panicked.

He shot Taco a longing glance, only fifteen feet away... All Nate had to do was walk away. "Don't beat yourself up over it," he said instead. "Let me take a look at it now that the water's off."

"No. I've already put you through so much. I can handle it from here."

He'd have to see that to believe it. "I'm happy to do it, ma'am," he said. *Resigned* to it might be a better word. He'd expected to come over to make his welcome known and head out. But he couldn't very well leave her stranded like this. What if it were Kayla needing a helping hand—not that she ever would have, she'd been an amazing woman. Still, that sealed his fate. "I'm Nate Talbert. Your neighbor," he offered, feeling off-kilter. He jerked his head toward the direction of his house, though it was well hidden behind a stand of oak and pine.

"You're our neighbor!" the kid exclaimed jumping around him. "And that's your horse! Woo-hoo!"

Nate looked from the freckled-faced kid to the mother. They had matching green eyes.

"It's nice to meet you," she said. "I'm Pollyanna McDonald and this is my son, Gilly."

"Aw, Mom, it's Gil."

"Excuse me, my bad," she said, rubbing his wet hair. "This is Gil."

Gil looked serious again. "No man of the house is s'posed to be called *Gilly*. That sounds like a baby."

Nate caught a shadow in Pollyanna's eyes. The woman was plain, but she had some expressive eyes. "You are exactly right," she said. "You are growing up on me."

Nate was distracted, and glad of it, as the dog bumped into him and tried to sniff at his jeans. The cone hindered him from getting his bulb of a nose as close as he wanted. Unable to understand it wasn't going to work, the animal kept trying, repeatedly bumping one side of the cone then the other against Nate's calf. That made the kid laugh and the mother grow flustered.

"Gil, take Bogie around front to play," she said. As if one too many things were out of her control, she snatched up her long, dripping hair and twisted it nervously. Water poured to the ground.

"But, Mom—"

"No buts. Mr. Talbert doesn't need to be harassed while he's trying to help."

The kid looked like he was going to protest again, then thought better of it and reached for the dog. "Can I come watch you fix the pipe in a few minutes?" he called, using his knee to hoist the dog securely into his arms as he lumbered under his load toward the house.

Nate couldn't very well say no, so he gave a curt nod, which made the boy light up. "Awesome," he yelped just as the dog hit him in the chin with its cone. "Hold on, Bogie," he urged gently, then, shifting his heavy load, he disappeared around the corner of the house.

"You may rue the day we moved in next door," Pollyanna McDonald said, slinging her hair over her shoulder and planting her hands on her hips. Her tools jingled.

Looking at her, Nate wasn't sure how to react, so he didn't. "I'll take that look now," was all he said, and strode toward the porch. He was soaked from his knees to his Stetson, but that didn't even compare to the condition of his neighbor. He didn't know how long she'd stood in the spray before he'd arrived, but obviously it had been longer than needed. Even above the jangle of her tools he could hear her shoes and jeans squelching as she trailed behind him.

He felt bad for her, losing her husband and all, but frankly, he wasn't too keen on the idea of a neighbor who didn't even know, so to speak, "how to get out of the rain." It didn't bode well. Not at all.

So that was her new neighbor. Not much of a talker, Polly thought as she watched him stride into her house. Of course, what man would be under the circumstances? She'd yanked the poor guy right into the water—probably ruined his hat. She couldn't be any more mortified. Needing his help was bad enough. That she'd forced him to take a swim was just too much to think about.

She'd really made a mess of things. How could she not have known how to shut the water off? She hadn't even thought to ask the real-estate agent where it was. She'd never needed to turn the main line of water off in her entire life. Still, any ninny should have known how to find a lever and yank!

Taking a calming breath, she pushed away the negative feelings and followed Nate Talbert through the doorway into her house. Not knowing how to turn off a main water valve was a small thing and, though, for a moment she'd let it get to her, she refused to allow it to continue having an upper hand.

The utility room was much calmer. The water had

stopped, Gil and Bogie were outside, and Pepper, having had his bath, had flown into another part of the house.

Nate removed his hat and hooked it on the end of the curtain rod vacated by Pepper. He pulled the washing machine farther out from the wall and sloshed through the two inches of water to study the situation.

The man was a good six-three, maybe -four, and his shoulders were broad, making it tough for him to squeeze into the tight space between the wall and the washer. He was a handsome man, a little hard-looking, with a firm mouth below prominent cheekbones and a Gregory Peck nose, a nice nose.

Not that she usually paid much attention to nice noses or how good-looking a man was. The fact that she'd noticed such a thing set her to feeling even more at odds with the entire situation. Grabbing a mop, she attacked the water that had flooded not only the utility room but a good portion of her kitchen. "I could call a plumber," she offered, really hating that this stranger was dealing with her problem. Not to mention how foolish he must think her.

He leaned forward, studying the pipe. "No need," he said, his words clipped. "I've got the right part over at my place. I'll just go get it and be back in a few minutes."

Polly clamped her mouth shut on the protest that begged to come out. He didn't look too happy, but he had offered. "If you're sure it's not too much trouble," she said instead. Why she bothered was a mystery since he was already striding out the door. He was heading down the steps before she'd set her mop to the side and followed him outside.

In a swift, easy movement of a man used to maneuvering a barbed-wire fence, he bent and gracefully swooped through the middle strands without using his hands to hold the wire apart.

With the same amount of ease he swung into the saddle and rode away. Polly thought of the Lone Ranger and felt like all that was missing was a "High-yo, Silver."

There was no wasted energy about Nate Talbert. In movements or in words.

Actually, that suited Polly just fine. It wasn't as if she was going to be asking the man for help on a regular basis.

Spinning away, she hurried to clean up the watery disaster. The least she could do for him if he was going to work in there was make the utility room habitable.

That is, if he came back.

Given a few minutes to digest the circus he'd walked into, he might get home and decide calling a plumber wasn't such a bad idea after all.

Thirty minutes later Nate had just started working on the broken valve when the kid tromped into the room. "Hey, Nate—"

"That's Mr. Talbert to you, young man," rang out from somewhere in the other room, causing the boy's ears to turn pink.

"Mr. Talbert," he started over, hopping from foot to foot. "Can I watch?"

Nate's first inclination was to say no. He'd already denied the mother's offer to help and been glad when she hadn't given him any argument about it. The last thing he needed was her hovering over him while he tried to work. It was a little too personal for his taste. But the kid. He was a different story. His earlier statement hung in the air between them. He was the man of the house.

"That'd be fine," Nate said tersely, immediately going back to work.

Gil scooted right in there, plopped his elbows on the washing machine and leaned in as far as he could, watching Nate over the control panel. He wasn't terribly tall, but tall enough.

The kid asked what everything was and why it needed to be done the way he was doing it. Nate explained on a need-to-know basis, figuring if the kid had the wherewithal to come up with the question, then he would retain the information better. Because, Nate agreed with Gil, the kid did need to know these things.

Twenty minutes later, almost finished, Nate started tightening the new connections, when he met the kid's longing gaze. "You want to give this a tug and finish it off? It's your house." The offer lit Gil's eyes like a Roman candle. Struck by the intense will he saw in the boy's eyes, Nate knew he couldn't turn away from the fact that they were his neighbors and it wouldn't hurt him to give the boy some encouragement and direction.

"All right!" he whooped, and scrambled to squeeze between Nate and the washing machine. Grabbing hold of the wrench, he pulled, then pushed it around. Nate gave him a little help with the final tightening.

"It's good to go," Nate said when it wouldn't go any farther.

"Yep, it's good to go," Gil echoed, puffing his chest out and looking up at him.

Nate had an urge to squeeze the boy's thin shoulder. But he didn't. Instead he gave him room to move away. "Are you going to wash the first load?"

Gil spun around. "Me? That's girl stuff."

Nate lifted a brow. "The man of the house needs to know how to wash his own clothes." It had been a hard lesson learned. Having a doting mother and then a doting wife, he'd made a mess of things for a while.

Gil's forehead crinkled. "You know how to wash your own clothes?"

"Yup." Nate's gaze snagged on Pollyanna's as she came through the double doors into the utility room. She'd changed into dry clothes and towel dried her previously drenched hair. She was pretty in a soft way. "I'm all done here." He was suddenly more than ready to get back home.

She leaned against the door frame and watched him push the washer closer to the wall, Gil helping.

"Mom. Nat— Mr. Talbert says I should learn to wash my own clothes."

Wiping his hands on a rag Pollyanna had given him earlier, Nate looked from child to mother. Dry, they really were a matched pair in more ways than their green eyes. They had the same wavy hair, like the warm color of Bogie's cinnamon coat, and both had a dusting of freckles across their noses.

"I think that'd be a grand idea. We can start with

your jeans and all those towels you use when you take your baths. How about you run up and feed your animals right now and I'll get your supper on the table."

"Sure! Hey, Mr. Talbert, you wanna stay for supper? Can he, Mom?" He was hopping from one foot to the other again and Nate got the idea that the boy was in constant motion.

Nate shook his head, catching the flash of hesitation in Pollyanna's eyes. "No, that's okay." He was as against the idea as she obviously was.

She blushed and her good manners took over in an instant as her expression shifted into a smile. Unsure, but a smile. "Oh, please stay. After what we've put you through, I owe you something for all your trouble."

She didn't owe him anything. "No trouble." He was already reaching for his hat. "But I've got my own chores to finish up." He saw the disappointment in the boy's eyes and the relief in hers as he strode the short steps to the back door.

It was one thing to help out, but the last thing he needed or they needed was to get too close.

To his credit, the boy didn't protest but once, and Nate couldn't help noticing that his mother's hand on his shoulder and a quick shake of her head halted anything else he might have said. At the door, Nate tipped his wet hat and left them there, mother and child, and at their feet, the dog. And somewhere behind them the bird singing, "Jesus loves Pepper, oh, yes, He does."

An odd bunch that made Nate intensely aware of all the dreams he'd laid to rest when he lost Kayla.

Only days before he'd prayed for the Lord to send him a miracle to help him cope with the leftovers of his life… He had a bad feeling he was going to need that miracle even more now, because his neighbors were acute reminders of exactly how empty his life had become.

Chapter Three

The day after the washing-machine fiasco Gil woke up talking about their new neighbor. He was talking about Nate Talbert even as his ride picked him up for school and they drove away. Mule Hollow shared a school with a couple of other small communities. It was about twenty miles from town. Polly and the mother of one of the other boys had joined forces and started a carpool. As she watched the car disappear down the lane, she breathed a sigh of relief.

She didn't exactly know how to take her son's sudden and immediate infatuation with the gruff cowboy.

She didn't have time to think about it long since a trail of cars turned in her drive almost immediately.

In the lead was the pink 1958 Caddy that belonged to Lacy Matlock. Lacy had the top down, and she started waving the moment she spotted Polly on the porch. Polly wasn't sure she'd ever met anyone as full of life and love of the Lord as Lacy. They were about the same age, but next to Lacy, Polly felt a bit like a tarnished penny.

Within seconds Lacy pulled to a halt and the truck following her did, too. The three older women who climbed out of it were Mule Hollow's very heart and soul. They'd single-handedly come up with a plan to save their town by advertising for would-be wives. The idea had picked up; women had answered the call. Day after day there was one less lonesome cowboy riding the range around town.

When Polly had first heard about the town, she almost hadn't believed the story. But it was true. The town once bustling with life had started dying when the oil boom busted and the families had to move off to find work. Not close enough to anything to attract new families, all that had remained were the old-timers and the cowboys. Things were changing due to the efforts of these three ladies and Lacy.

And Polly had chosen to move here because she felt drawn to be a part of the effort. She also felt that it was a great place for a B and B. When she'd found this Victorian for sale she'd believed it was a sign that this was the place to make her dreams come true.

Within minutes of their arrival, Polly's kitchen was a flurry of action as they all set to help her unpack the huge amount of boxes. She had furniture that would still be delivered after she got the upstairs painted, but that was going to take her at least a couple of weeks. For now, when the kitchen was unpacked she would be box free for a little while. That was a good feeling.

"You should take the doors off those cabinets,"

Esther Mae Wilcox said a half hour later. She stood studying the cabinets, her red head tilted to the side and her index finger on her chin. "You have all this stunning glass. You shouldn't hide it behind doors."

"That's a great idea," Polly agreed from where she stood barefoot on the counter. She loved Depression glass and had collected an overabundance of it. It was going to come in handy now that she was opening the bed-and-breakfast. "If I remove these pesky doors it'll not only make the room look like a rainbow of color, but be convenient for me, too."

The room had twelve-foot ceilings. The cabinets went all the way up, which was one reason she was standing barefoot on the counter. It beat going up and down a ladder as Esther Mae handed her dish after dish.

From all corners of the room everyone offered their agreement.

"I just love Depression glass," Esther Mae continued. She pulled a plate from the box and admired it before handing it up to Polly. "Although, I think the name is oddly off since there is nothing depressing about it."

"It was made during the Depression," Norma Sue Jenkins said from inside the walk-in pantry where she was working. "That's depressing enough!"

"Well, I know that," Esther Mae huffed. "I lived through it as a kid, too, you know. Maybe that's why I love to look at it so much. There just isn't anything prettier than a bunch of colored glass."

"I agree," Lacy said.

Polly handled the dainty plate with care. "My grandmother got me started with my infatuation with it. Those green Vaseline dishes were hers. I started collecting the Depression glass because it looked similar and I loved the colors, especially the pink and blue dishes. And the lemon," she smiled. "Who am I kidding? I love them all."

"Me, too." Esther Mae chuckled. "You know, if you hold a black light to the Vaseline glass it fires because of the uranium in it." She held the bright green candy dish to her. "That means it glows in black light," she said for anyone who might not know what she was talking about.

Polly took it from her when she held it up to her. "My gram, she keeps hers in a special cabinet my granddad built her. He installed black lighting, and when I was a kid she loved to turn off the lights and show me how her dishes glowed."

"Where do your grandparents live?" Norma Sue asked as she came out of the pantry. She was a robust woman with an infectious smile that filled out her plump face. Polly had a feeling that anything Norma Sue set out to do got done.

"They moved to Arizona because of my granddad's allergies. We don't get to see them as much now and I really miss them. I almost moved out there to open my place. But I wanted to stay in Texas. Just wanted to get out of Dallas."

"And we are so glad you did. What about your parents?" Adela Ledbetter-Green asked, setting a blue glass on the table beside a group of matching pieces.

She was a darling wisp of a woman, quieter than her two friends, and though she was a widow in her early seventies she'd recently married her longtime sweetheart. Polly thought that was both romantic and a bit sad, too, thinking about how life moves forward. Her Marc slipped into her thoughts, bringing with him that mixture of emotions. With God's help and her determination to make Marc proud of her, she was moving forward without him beside her…but to remarry— The very idea set alarms off in her heart.

"My parents," she said, pushing the idea of remarrying out of her mind, "live in Brenham, Texas. You know, the home of Blue Bell ice cream."

"I just love that ice cream!" Esther Mae exclaimed. "You know that homemade vanilla can't be beat. Of course, my Hank, he's a Rocky Road fella. 'Course, I can't eat too much of it since I've started my exercise program."

Norma Sue coughed. "I saw three cartons of the stuff in your freezer when I went to get ice for my tea yesterday. There was hardly any room in there for ice."

Esther Mae harrumphed. "It was on sale, three for ten dollars. I couldn't pass up a deal like that."

Lacy paused from wiping drawers, her blue eyes sparkling. She caught Polly's gaze, winked, then went back to work. Polly had realized soon after meeting the three older ladies that Norma Sue and Esther Mae played off of each other like a stand-up act. They bantered and bickered good naturedly almost constantly, while Adela threw in a comment every once in a while to gently steer them back in from chasing rabbits to the conversation at hand. A person couldn't help smiling. Listening to them made her think of her grandparents, who also enjoyed a good argument.

Esther Mae was handing Polly a bowl when Norma Sue came over and looked up at her.

"So, what do you think about your neighbor?"

The sudden change of subject brought Polly up short. Up until yesterday she'd only seen her neighbor coming and going in the distance that separated their driveways. Her home sat up on a hill, and though she couldn't see his home because it was screened by a stand of oak trees, his long driveway was very visible. "Well, I only just met him yesterday." She glanced around the room to find everyone watching her the way Gil eyed his birthday presents before he opened them.

"You mean, he actually came over?" Esther Mae gasped.

Polly wasn't too excited about revealing her embarrassing moment, but she told them, anyway.

When she finished telling the tale everyone looked shocked.

"Our Nate did that?" Norma Sue asked.

"Yes. Poor man probably wishes I'd never moved in beside him."

"Oh, no, dear," Adela assured her. "This is a good thing."

Esther Mae was handing Pollyanna a gold vase, but she absentmindedly yanked her arm back, leaving Polly grasping at air. "It really is. I was beginning to worry about that boy. Why, I honestly didn't think he would come over here and introduce himself to you. He's become such a hermit."

"Don't worry about him," Adela said. "He has to act in his own time. He hasn't been one to offer help in the past three years because he needed the time to heal."

"That's right," Lacy agreed. "We've got to keep the faith that he's coming around. He's helped with a couple of festivals lately. That's progress."

Norma Sue shook her wiry gray hair. "But only in the setting up of them. He didn't come near town during the actual events. Not even the Christmas program."

"That's right, but we've understood." Adela looked about the room, her gaze coming to rest on Pollyanna. "He's had to take his time, move at his own pace, and we've tried not to interfere or push. You and I understand that," she explained. Her brilliant blue eyes were full of compassion. "No one can truly understand what it means to lose your soul mate like those who've experienced it."

A lump rose in Polly's throat. Nate Talbert was a widower.

"I'm so sorry," she said, knowing all too well the words were inadequate. Polly hated to think about it, but one half of every couple would someday have to face the loss of the other, it was a part of living. Still, she wouldn't wish it on anyone. The knowledge that her neighbor had borne such a loss both saddened her and linked her to him as it did with Adela. It was like being members of a club you had no desire to be initiated into but couldn't get out of.

"God's blessed me, dear. God has given us resilient

hearts, and you may not see it yet, but you and Nate can have room in your hearts to love again."

A shadow fell over Polly's heart. "I'm really happy for you, Adela, but I'm not looking for love again."

"Of course you are," Esther Mae exclaimed. "You're too young and you have that wonderful son who needs a daddy."

"Esther Mae," Norma Sue barked, censure in her tone.

"Don't you 'Esther Mae' me," the feisty redhead snapped, her gaze lifted to Polly. Her voiced gentled. "You can't limit the Lord like that, Pollyanna."

Polly crouched down on the counter and patted Esther Mae's hand. "It's okay, it's not like that. I'm okay, Gil's okay. I came to Mule Hollow to open a business—*not* for one of your cowboys. I'll leave them for someone else. Really. God's blessed me with the love of an amazing man and for a little while I had more than I could ever hope or dream of… That kind of love couldn't happen twice. And well, I don't have any desire to mess up such a perfect memory. That's the main reason I'll never marry again."

"The main reason—you have more?" Esther Mae asked.

Polly swallowed down the fear, the doubts that always rushed to the surface if she let her guard down. She nodded, not trusting her voice at first. "Oh, yes," she managed to say after a moment. "I have more."

The afternoon after meeting his new neighbors, the boy and his dog showed up when Nate was unloading feed. He'd ridden his bike over, and Bogie was panting like a locomotive as they huffed around the bend and into the yard. "Hey, Nate!" Gil called, hopping from his bike while it was still moving, then pulling it to a stop. "What's in the bags?"

"Feed," Nate grunted, hefting two at a time onto the palettes in the corner of the barn. It wasn't as if he could ignore the boy, even though he had a bad feeling about the entire situation. Off and on all morning he'd rehashed the emotions he'd felt the day before, being around Gil and his mother. He felt a sense of connection to them in one sense but he also felt an overwhelming need to maintain his distance. He'd become almost accustomed to being disconnected from everything. Sure, he'd asked for intervention, but truthfully, the Lord was going to have to intervene with his attitude, too, or it wasn't happening. Some bruises ran too deep.

But none of that was the kid's fault, and Nate was smart enough to know that the strain he felt around the boy had more to do with how much he'd wanted kids with Kayla than anything about Gil. He wouldn't be much of a man if he took it out on the fresh-faced boy.

"I can help," Gil offered, kicking the stand to his bike down and leaving it in the door of the barn. Bogie, too tuckered out to be curious, dropped like a rock to his belly in the dust.

Nate felt his gut twist but nodded as he hefted another load. "Tell you what. How 'bout you climb into the bed of the truck and push bags off the top there down to me." Nate didn't figure the slight boy could lift a fifty-pound bag, he'd seen him struggle to carry Bogie, but maybe he could shove one in his direction.

Face set in determination, Gil scampered up into the truck and reached for the bag on the top of the stack. With a grunt he pulled. When nothing happened he climbed behind the bags and shoved. The bag rewarded him by sliding to the bed with a thud.

"Good job," Nate said, and meant it. He tugged it to him and tossed it to the stack. Gil already had his shoulder pressed to the next bag, his expression ripe with the effort. They worked for almost thirty minutes, and Nate couldn't help admire the boy's hard work. When the truck was empty, Gil hopped to the ground.

"Got anything else to do?"

Nate had been about to clean out some stalls, and though he figured Gil would run at the sound of that, he offered it up.

"Woo-hoo! Gimme a shovel— I use a shovel, right?"

Nate almost laughed. Almost.

"Maybe you need to give your mother a call and let her know where you are first." Pollyanna might get worried when Gil didn't show up for so long.

"Maybe I better. You know how moms are."

Nate motioned to the phone hanging on the wall next to the tack room. "She wants to talk to you, Nate," he called after only a moment on the line.

Nate took the phone. "Yes?" he said, watching Gil hop around like he was prone to do.

"Are you sure you don't mind him helping? If he's in the way, please just send him home."

Her voice was soft and he pictured her gentle green eyes looking pensive as she said the words. He was struck by the image and startled by how much he felt the need to reassure her. "He's a good helper. If you don't mind, I'd appreciate the help."

There was a long pause, as if she was weighing the validity of his assurance. He added, "A boy living in the country needs to know how to muck out a stall." Her chuckle startled him a little, like another pinprick on a toughened callus.

"I'm sure you're right about that," she said. "If you're sure, then I know he would love it."

"Yes, ma'am. I'll send him home in a couple of hours."

"Nate, thank you," she said, before he could hang up.

"No need," he said, more than a little uncomfortable as he pressed the disconnect button.

Two hours later he sent Gil and Bogie home. He wondered if Pollyanna would thank him when her son walked into her clean house smelling worse than the stalls he'd cleaned. Nate found himself smiling as he watched the kid race his bike around the bend with the dog in hot pursuit, holding his head high in order to keep his feet on the ground.

Something told Nate that as long as Gil came home smiling, Pollyanna McDonald wouldn't care if her son stunk like a polecat.

Chapter Four

It was only seven in the morning but Polly had been up since five. Rubbing her tired neck, she walked from her office.

In the two hours, she'd sent off approval of her Web site and accepted a couple of reservations for midsummer from an online booking directory she was listed with. She'd also finally decided on the bedding she wanted in the four guest rooms, and had ordered it quickly so she wouldn't change her mind again. At least now she would be able to choose her paint colors. That was a relief. She had a lot on her mind and hadn't been sleeping well. The B and B had to be a success for so many reasons. Besides making Marc proud and fulfilling their dream for Gil, she needed to feel in control of something in her life again. Each thing she marked off her list helped.

She and Marc had had some savings, but they'd also had a good life-insurance policy. Marc hadn't taken his responsibility lightly, especially with his love of extreme sports. However, Polly wanted to stand on her own two feet. She'd invested Marc's money and kept enough back to use as seed money for the business, and she was trying to live off of their other savings until she had an income from the bed-and-breakfast.

Marc's insurance money was funding their dream and, invested wisely, it would always give her and Gil a cushion to fall back on. The bed-and-breakfast showed great promise. Of course, being a worrier, she still feared it could fail. But as far as she could tell it was a healthy fear that kept her aggressive.

Coming around the corner, she spotted Bogie in his usual morning pose, sitting on the back of the couch, looking regally funny in his collar. She was convinced the dog thought he was a cat. Of course, his oddities weren't exclusive to him. The shar-pei breed wasn't fond of water, they batted balls around on the floor with paws cupped like a cat's, and because of their huge protector instinct, they loved to climb to a high spot. It gave them a lookout advantage, she assumed. Bogie preferred the couch but climbed up on anything available. If chairs were left pulled away from anything he climbed onto it—the table, vanity or desk—and proudly kept watch. But climbing wasn't his only extracurricular activity. Sometimes he took things. Before she caught him on top of her desk, she'd thought she was going crazy when things would go missing and turn up in weird places. Like her pocketbook behind the corner chair, or her hairbrush behind the toilet!

The breed also had a natural instinct to bond with a family unit. It was this reason her parents had given them the wrinkled pup. They knew she worried about Gil's emotional state since losing his daddy and they wanted to relieve her a little by giving him something with a huge capacity to love and protect.

What they hadn't realized was that shar-peis didn't have tremendous life expectancies…eight, ten years maybe. Polly hated the thought of Gil bonding with something so strongly only to lose it. She knew the fear was also for herself.

And yet with Bogie, Pepper and Gil's two turtles they were on their way to raising a farm. Add in the goat Gil wanted and the cow she wanted, and she seriously was going to have more to worry about. If any one of those animals died, she was going to have to watch Gil suffer again.

Death cut deeper than she could bear. Fear of it could be paralyzing…even for a woman with a strong faith in the Lord. If she could, she would protect Gil from ever having to experience it again.

A flash of color caught her eye and she looked up just in time to see Gil whizzing down the banister. He let out a whoop and landed on his feet with a thud. Just the luck of a worrywart like her, her son was part mountain goat. And fearless like his father.

"Gil, you keep sliding down that banister and you're going to hurt yourself. You've got to stop that," she admonished. Her heart was thudding.

"Mom, it's fun."

Fun. That was the name of the game when it came

to Gil. Again, just like it had been for his father. Polly smiled despite herself, her heart swelling with love and fear at the same time. Marc would have slid down the banister with him…while she was telling him to stop. "We'll talk about it later. You ready for breakfast before Rose picks you up for school?"

"Oh, yeah, I'm *starrr-vin' Marrr-vin,*" Gil drawled, using one of Marc's favorite sayings. Hearing Gil, or Pepper, come out with one of Marc's lines always made her smile. She took a deep breath and fought off the burn of tears. What was wrong with her this morning? Tired, she decided as she watched Gil play a game of tag with Bogie. The dog all but tripped over his collar trying to get to Gil and rolled off the couch, landing in a heap. The noise stirred Pepper to life, and from upstairs, safely ensconced in the large cage where he ended and began each day, Pepper began singing "Jesus Loves Pepper" to Gil's turtles, his very own captive audience.

The song was God's perfect timing as Polly was reminded by the childlike voice drifting down to her that, despite her worries, all was well.

She was convinced God used Pepper's small voice to help calm her and remind her that she was not alone in raising her son.

She blinked away the sting of tears and sent up a quick silent prayer of thanks for both the reassurance and for Gil's continued safety.

They were doing okay. They really, really were.

She thought of Nate Talbert. The man had let Gil help him for the past couple of days and it had made

Gil so happy. He'd come rushing in the first day looking like Pig Pen and smelling like one, too. But how
happy he'd been. Country life suited him.

And that was an answer to prayer. It was also something that demanded acknowledgment.

Thanks to the girls, her kitchen was ready for business, and Nate Talbert looked like a man who could
use a home-cooked meal.

"So the trip was good?" Nate asked his mother the
minute he answered the phone and heard it was her.
He'd been expecting her to call the moment she and
his dad arrived home from their cruise.

"Alaska was as splendid as I thought it would be,"
she said, then paused. Nate could hear his dad in the
background telling her something. "Your father says
you should go. And I agree."

Nate stared out his office window and shook his
head. "Tell Dad I'll let the two of you do all the traveling in this family."

His mother sighed. He didn't have to see her face
to know she was fighting a mixture of exasperation and
sorrow. He hoped she'd let it go. "Nate, honey, you always wanted to travel."

Yeah, with Kayla. They'd planned to travel as soon
as they had the time. Turned out they didn't have any of
that.

"Your brother will go with you if you don't want to
travel alone."

"Mom, stop." He didn't want to hurt her, but she had
to stop. She'd just this year started hinting that it was

time for him to start dating. Start traveling. Start living. It was always something that began with *start* or *try.*

By *trying,* she meant *move forward,* and her high hope was that he would meet a nice woman and re-marry. Nate had a real problem with people wanting this for him. Still, she was his mother, and she wanted grandchildren. And since she'd given up on his brother ever settling down, Nate was still her best hope. Plus, she wanted Nate to be happy again.

"I'll be up to bring that load of cattle in two weeks," he said, not answering her plea. There was no sense lying to her.

She sighed into the phone. "Oh, all right. I'll tell your brother."

"Thanks, Mom. That'll save me calling him." Nate's brother, Tyler, ran the family ranch operation outside Fort Worth. Their dad had suffered a light heart attack a few months back and was trying to slow down and enjoy life a little bit. This cruise had been part of the plan. Nate's mother thought grandchildren running around would help him adjust to not working so hard. Nate felt guilty for not being able to give her what she wanted. But life wasn't fair, and people didn't always get what they wanted. Still, he felt bad for his mother. She deserved grandchildren. He was going to have a heart-to-heart with his brother when he went home.

He and his mother discussed the trip for a few more minutes before saying their goodbyes. She always ended her phone conversations with "I'll be praying for you, dear."

Nate figured his mother's prayers had helped him through his worst times. Hanging up the phone, he bowed his head and prayed for her. She was the best woman Nate knew, and she deserved to have her heart's desire.

He was heading out the door when the phone rang again. Thinking his mother had forgotten to tell him something, which she usually did when she called him, he snatched up the headset. "Did you forget something?" he teased.

"You could say that."

Pollyanna's chuckle through the line was an unexpected surprise. "You're not my mother." *Real sharp, Talbert.*

"No. Sorry."

"I just hung up," he explained, and moved on quickly. "Did you need something?"

"Yes, actually. I need you."

Chapter Five

That evening, with dread knotting in his stomach, Nate strode up the five steps flanked by two large pots of what looked like tulips that hadn't bloomed yet. He quickly knocked on the screen door before he lost his nerve and fled. After letting Gil tag along for the past couple of days, Pollyanna had called and insisted that he let her cook him supper. Nate had finally agreed to the invitation, however reluctantly. When Gil had come by after school, the boy had been over-the-top excited, and that had done away with any thoughts Nate had toyed with about reneging.

Pinching the bridge of his nose, he willed his insides to settle down. The very idea of sitting at another woman's table had him feeling as nauseated as he'd been the first time he'd been kicked in the gut by a disgruntled heifer. He told himself it had nothing to do with the silky way Pollyanna's voice had pleaded with him over the phone. Or the way he kept remembering how her eyes practically talked out loud, they were so expressive.

Nate knocked again. No one came but he knew by the soft laughter drifting from somewhere inside the house that they were home and just hadn't heard him.

Swiping his hat from his head, he tried another route. "Hello," he called, pulling open the screen. Unanswered, he stepped just inside. An impressive staircase wound upward in front of him. His gaze followed it up. One side of the railing detoured at the second floor, but the other railing never broke as it wound in a wide smooth arch up to the third story…man, would that be one good ride. Curious about the rest of the house, he moved into the large living room. Second thoughts about intruding converged on him. He started to turn around and go back to the porch when Pollyanna's laughter rang out. The sheer delight of her laughter hooked him.

Eyes on the doorway at the end of the living room, he took a few more steps and almost tripped on a puppy leg.

The lazy dog was sleeping beneath an end table, sprawled on his back, his relaxed face a scrunched-up mass of wrinkles inside the "lamp shade" collar.

"—they're gonna like it here, Mama. Bo's smiling. See? And look at Sylvie go," Gil called out excitedly.

"Pepper, too. Pepper, too!"

"Yes, Pepper, you can watch, too." Pollyanna laughed. "I think Bo's letting Sylvie win because he loves her desperately."

Pollyanna's voice was husky with laughter as Nate stuck his head into the room. Mother and son were sitting on the floor of the kitchen side by side turned slightly away from him. They were watching two turtles striding—well, at least they were striding as fast as two turtles could stride—across the floor toward what looked like a red string of candy licorice. A *Twizzler.* The bright green cockatiel was perched on Gil's shoulder, doing a wild dance as he watched the race. It had to be one of the oddest things Nate'd ever seen. Before Nate could speak up, the bird cocked its orange-spotted head and pinned its beady little eyes on him. Instantly the feathers on its head fanned forward as the bird lifted one foot and pointed it at him.

"Stranger! Stranger!" it screeched, then flew straight at Nate.

Caught off guard, Nate whipped back to avoid the dive-bombing bird. Too late he realized that a disoriented Bogie had sprung into action, rushing in behind him—very effectively cutting his feet right out from under him.

'Bout summed up his day, Nate thought as his feet sailed out from under him and he hit the floor like a pile of rocks.

And there he lay. A green bird circling overhead, a fat, wrinkled pooch bumping into him with its odd plastic helmet, and a laughing boy and his emerald-eyed mother standing over him.

"Are you okay?" Pollyanna blinked big eyes at him.

Nate wasn't sure if it was because he'd smacked his head on the hardwood floor, but he just stared up at her like an idiot. She really did have the most dazzling eyes.

And a cute, tiny dimple beside her lips.

"Pepper gotcha! Pepper gotcha good." Gil giggled, doubling over.

Nate sat up and rubbed the back of his head.

"Gil, be nice," Pollyanna scolded, but Nate saw the corners of her lips twitch.

"It's all right." He grinned at Gil, then up at Pollyanna. "It's my due for coming into your house uninvited. Besides, boys are born with an odd sense of humor."

That made her smile. Not just smile, the woman's eyes lit up and twinkled like a thousand stars. "Yes. They are," she said, her gaze settling on Gil like a caress.

That look shot longing through Nate as sharp as a hunter's arrow.

"He is truly a carbon copy of his daddy," she said, her gaze returning to Nate. "Never knew what Marc was going to come out with next. Here, let me help you up."

She reached for Nate's arm. Her touch was soft and sent a shock wave through him that knocked the breath out of him. This woman had loved well. Pollyanna McDonald was the kind of woman who loved with everything in her. Death, and space and time couldn't diminish it. At least, that was the impression he got of her.

They had that in common. In a way the idea made him sad for her.

The less you loved, the less you hurt.

"Gil, go find Pepper and put him in his cage. He's too excited to be zooming around the house right now," she said, still tugging on Nate's arm.

Bogie bumped into him with his lamp shade, trying unsuccessfully to lick Nate's face. The whiff of awful doggie breath shook the cobwebs out of Nate's head and made him thankful the dog couldn't get any closer. Pollyanna was tugging on him pretty hard, so he helped her out by standing up. He didn't want her pulling a back muscle.

"Come, sit here," she demanded, sweeping him into the kitchen and pushing him onto a bar stool. "Are you sure you're okay? I invite you to dinner and my circus tries to do you in." Her face was now a work of anxiety.

His pride was injured, but it would only hurt it more to mention it. "I'm fine. Were you racing turtles?" He glanced at the two turtles eating a strip of candy.

"We sure were. Sylvie and Bo love to race for candy. And as you saw, Pepper is their cheerleader. Those two will really turn on the juice for a cherry Twizzler." She grimaced comically.

And Nate laughed.

It happened so unexpectedly, that he froze.

The look that washed over Nate after he laughed was so stricken, so lost, that Polly knew instinctively what had happened. Her first impression of Nate had been that of a man still floundering from the loss of his wife. She understood this all too well.

"Is that the first time?" she asked, knowing the answer before he spoke it.

His brows dipped. "The first time?"

"That you've laughed since your wife died?" She knew it had been three years since his wife died.

"Pretty much."

His expression said for her to drop it, that she'd stepped where she shouldn't. Then suddenly the emotion was gone. The clouds she'd glimpsed in his eyes vanished, as if the sun had come out. She wasn't fooled. She'd been there…she knew behind the dark, impersonal eyes she was looking into now that emotions were raging. She recognized a protective device when she saw it. She'd used it herself many times over the past two years.

For a moment she couldn't say anything, the recognition so acute that she felt her heart clutch inside her chest.

Gil's anxious voice calling out to Pepper broke the moment, followed by the sound of scraping and shuffling. Nate heard it, too, his head whipping around. The call had come from above them, drifting in from outside through the open screen door.

Gil was on the roof!

They reacted together. Bounding through the house and onto the porch, they raced down the steps and jogged clear of the roof line. Polly's heart thundered. Surely the sound of Gil's voice had just drifted out to them from an open window. But she knew she was wrong before she spotted her son. And Pepper.

The bird was perched on top of one of the three dormers on the tiny second-story ledge, though it wasn't Pepper Polly's gaze locked on. It was Gil.

Her son was creeping toward Pepper on the steep roof, talking soothingly to the terrified bird. Polly's first thought was at least they weren't on the third story—but the second story was scary enough for her. It was nothing more than a thin lip.

"Gilly," she called before regaining her faculties and registering that startling him wasn't the best option. It wasn't Gil who reacted badly to her shout, but Pepper. The scared bird flew straight up as if shot from a cannon, then frantically swooped downward a foot before flying over Gil's head and out into the open, aiming straight for the woods at least two hundred yards behind the house.

"Mom, whad'ya go and do that for?" Gil shouted, spinning around to watch his beloved bird disappearing. Polly's heart dropped when he teetered momentarily.

"Gilbert Marcus McDonald!" she shouted. "What do you think you're doing? Sit down right this minute before you fall off that roof and break your neck!"

Gil stared down at her, his little face bright as the orange spots on Pepper's cheeks. "*Mom,* it's only a roof. Pepper's gone and it's all my fault. I left the window open."

Polly worried for Pepper. The bird was terrified of the outdoors and with good reason—he had no idea how to survive. But her priority was getting her little daredevil out of his latest escapade. Without freaking out!

Nate touched her arm, then took a step forward, his eyes locked on Gil. "We'll get Pepper back, Gil." His voice was calm, but with enough firmness it drew Gil's attention. And Polly's.

One look at his eyes locked on her son and the rising swell of panic eased inside of Polly. Like the lull in a storm, it gave her a moment to get a grip. She thanked the Lord that he was here.

"But first, Gil," he continued, "you have to turn and walk back to that window. Can you do that?"

"Sure I can."

Polly would have laughed at Gil's insulted tone if she hadn't been so scared. Instead, she held her breath, watching and moving along with him as he walked the roof without wobbling. She should have grown used to his "adventures." There had been enough of them, but she hadn't. Every time she found him doing something like this she worried. Just like she'd done with Marc. He'd loved living life full throttle, out on the edge. Dirt bikes, speed boats, drag racing…skydiving. Anything that went fast held Marc in thrall.

She pushed the thoughts away, her gaze riveted to Nate as he took every step Gil took, his eyes glued to her son, ready to catch him if he should slip. When Gil climbed safely into his bedroom window, Nate actually heaved a sigh of relief and met her gaze.

"He made it. Just like he said he would."

If she hadn't been so distraught, Polly might have sighed herself from the sweet way Nate had handled the situation, but as it was, she frowned. "My son is going to give me gray hair before I reach thirty!"

"Are you okay?" Nate turned his full attention on Polly, his eyes full of concern.

She gave him a weak smile. "I should be used to stunts like this. He takes after his father, a born dare-devil. I almost didn't buy this house because of the multiple levels." She bit her lip. "But it was so perfect for a bed-and-breakfast. Now I think maybe I should have passed—"

"He's a boy."

Like that said it all, Polly thought. Of course, he was right. Marc had said the same thing, she'd just over-reacted. Like any mother would do, she added on in her defense. But then again, he was on the roof! At least, she would have made Marc proud, because she hadn't totally lost it. She sucked in a lungful of fresh air. "I'm doing my best not to coddle him, but it goes against my nature," she admitted. "Since Marc died, I've really had to fight not to overprotect him. Marc always balanced my worries with comments like the one you just made. 'Rite of passage,' he would have said." She met Nate's eyes, her lip curving up on one side. "You helped."

"Don't sell yourself short. You'd have done fine on your own." His dark brows knitted together above serious eyes.

"Right. And I guess you missed my near hysterics. Gil would have been totally mortified for his new hero to see his mother lose it. You being here made me dig deep. I've been working on handling things more like a man would—like his father would have. I have to learn to do that. I have to." Polly shut her eyes. Gil was a little boy who was going to need her to be strong, not to coddle him. She couldn't make him afraid of life. Once more, as it had at least twice an hour for the past two years, Polly felt the enormous weight on her shoulders of being a single parent.

Her admiration had tripled for single parents when she'd suddenly found herself one.

Nate patted her shoulder. "You did fine."

Gil's footsteps pounded to the floor, after yet another trip down the banister. Now he came running through the doorway and skidded to a stop in front of them with Bogie pouncing along behind him.

"C'mon on, y'all," Gil said, dashing down the steps.

"Let's take my truck," Nate offered, turning away.

Polly watched him, Gil and Bogie charge across the yard to the truck. Nate yanked the back door of the cab open and helped Gil and Bogie scramble in. "You coming?" he called to Polly as he closed the door and reached for his own.

Only then did Polly realize she hadn't moved, absorbed watching him with Gil. A wave of loss washed over her for Marc, seeing him pick up a much smaller Gil and place him in his car seat. "Y-yes, sure." Unsettled, she hurried to the passenger's side and within moments they were speeding across the pasture toward the stand of trees. Fighting hard, she regained a semblance of her composure. Even though it had been two years, moments of grief hit like that, swift and sharp, triggered by the smallest of things. But she had other things to worry about right now. If Gil lost Pepper it would devastate him in more ways than she wanted to think about. Loss was not an easy thing. Maybe she'd surrounded her son with all these animals in the hopes that if one died the others would ease his pain. But it was a lie and she knew it....

She pushed the thought away. They would find

Pepper. She wouldn't have to face her son's anguish again. Not today.

She glanced over at Nate. His strong jaw was set just as it had been when he'd focused on Gil balanced on the edge of that roof. She let his presence comfort her.

If someone had told Nate yesterday that today he'd be in the pasture cockatiel hunting, he'd have told them they'd been in one too many rodeos. But here he was doing exactly that.

As he guided the truck along the trail through the trees he marveled at the turn his life had taken in the short few days since his neighbors had arrived.

Gil and his mother, with their faces upturned, were anxiously scanning the trees in search of their lost bird. He hoped they found it for Gil's sake. The poor kid was growing more and more agitated with every moment that the bird didn't show up.

When Gil glanced his way, Nate's heartstrings tugged at the desperation he saw there. "I think we need to walk," Nate said abruptly, settling his boot firmly on the brake.

"Yeah," Gil said, nodding hard and blinking back what Nate knew were tears. "I might hear him talking to himself because he's scared. You know how he gets, Mama."

"You're right. When he's scared, Pepper talks to anything that's around."

Nate could hear desperation cloaked in Pollyanna's soft words.

Gil grinned at her words and looked at Nate with too bright eyes. "That bird can *talk*. Nate, have you ever wanted to stuff a sock in a bird's beak?"

His earnest question took Nate by surprise and he laughed for the second time that day. It came out sounding more like a cough from sucking in too much dust.

Gil's eyebrows crinkled and his eyes sobered. "I'm serious. If you're ever around Pepper long enough, you'll know what I mean. My dad, he taught him how to talk, and, boy, was he a good teacher." His voice faltered and his gaze skittered back toward the trees. "We gotta find him." His voice cracked. "H-he hates being outside."

Nate met Pollyanna's worried gaze. This little bird had a deeper connection with the boy than he'd first realized. He had already stopped the truck and now he opened the door. "Come on, kiddo, let's find your bird."

"Come on, Mama," Gil boomed, sliding off the seat. Pollyanna and Bogie got out on the other side and they all met at the rear of the truck. With the loud sound of the diesel engine not blotting everything else out, the woods now seemed to echo with silence. Of course they weren't, there was the rush of wind through the leaves and, among other mellow sounds, the soft warble of a songbird. Not the right bird.

"I think we should walk and listen first," Pollyanna said. Gil nodded, already plodding forward. Bogie followed along behind him, holding his head up so his collar didn't hang on the tall grass.

"Just be careful to watch your step and stay on the

track first," Nate warned, feeling a wave of protection pass over him.

"Thank you," Pollyanna said, falling into step beside him, watching Gil race forward. "I seem to be saying that to you on a regular basis. But he loves that bird. Pepper was Marc's and if we've lost him, it will be terribly hard on Gil. I don't think I could bear it."

Again Nate felt an overwhelming wave of protection for mother and son. It swept over him so strongly he was stunned.

But then, he understood attachment very well.

"We'll find him," he promised, and realized that he hadn't said anything in three years that he meant more.

They hadn't gone more than twenty feet when he heard something that didn't fit with the still quiet of the woods. He touched Pollyanna's arm and pointed east.

"That's him!" she exclaimed, clapping her hands in her excitement and grabbing Nate in an exuberant hug. Her face was illuminated by delight as she squeezed him practically in half. Then as quickly as she'd grabbed him she let him go, backed up and turned pink. "Sorry," she mouthed, then called her son back from the opposite direction. "Gilly, come here."

Gil raced back to them. "Do you see him?"

The boy was so excited he didn't even complain that his mother had just called him Gilly.

"Listen." Nate walked in the direction he'd heard the tiny voice. They were all silent, listening hard, hearing nothing out of the ordinary at first. Then it came again. Faintly at first, then growing in desperation.

"Pepper, all right. Pepper, all right. Jesus loves Pepper. Gilbert loves Pepper. Gilbert. *Gilll*-bert! Gilbert—"

"Pepper!" Gil yelped with joy and dashed past Nate. Nate and Pollyanna jogged after him with Bogie grunting behind them. A loud whack told him that Bogie had hit a tree. Nate glanced over his shoulder, and sure enough the dog was pulling himself up off the ground looking dazed. He shook it off and resumed galloping after them, his wrinkled face a picture of joyous glee, his droopy lips jiggling with every step. The dog reminded Nate of a walrus on legs.

What a zoo Pollyanna had. Nate laughed again and followed Gil, anxious to do whatever it took to reunite Gil and his bird. Ahead of him mother and son had stopped and were listening as they searched the trees.

"Pepper, I love you, too," Gil called, and held up his arms.

And then it came, the desperation in the childlike voice vanished, replaced with pure elation. "Pepper loves Gilbert! Pepper *loves* Gilbert."

There was a flutter from among the canopy of green, then the small bird swooped from the trees shrieking with elation. He landed on Gil's head babbling faster than a magpie on fast-forward.

Gil and Pollyanna giggled in relief and delight, and Nate, well, he was grinning like a goof, never so relieved in all his life.

Chapter Six

Polly and Gil attended their first church service at the Mule Hollow Church of Faith on Sunday. She was ashamed to admit it, but since Marc's death she'd struggled to attend church services. Not because she held a grudge against the Lord. It was something else. Something she'd never ever anticipated. She'd struggled attending church because the place that she should be most comfortable was actually the place that accentuated her loss. So much so that she could hardly bear it.

After years of attending church as a happy couple, walking in as a single—even thinking about it—caused her insides to curl up. She'd thought maybe it was just because back home it was her home church. The church she and Marc had attended together. The church she'd been married in—and held his funeral in.

She'd hoped and prayed things would be different here. But as she and Gil walked into the sanctuary she knew nothing had changed. She felt immediately lonesome for Marc. It had nothing to do with the warm welcome she received. It was odd that she could be embraced by a community and still struggle with the issues of feeling alone, and lonely. She found herself wondering if Nate felt the same way.

Looking around, she was disappointed not to find him. In the few short days that she'd known him he'd come to her rescue so many times she was afraid she might get accustomed to his help. She knew that he'd solidified his place as Gil's hero when he'd helped find Pepper.

Polly pushed thoughts of him from her mind as she saw Lacy Matlock waving her forward. Polly propelled Gil down the aisle and they slid in beside her and her handsome husband, Clint. The adoration the two shared for each other was evident, and Polly wondered if they really knew how lucky they were. If they truly understood how blessed they were.

She hadn't until it was too late.

"So, how's it going?" Lacy whispered when the song leader stood and gave them the hymnal page.

"Good," Polly whispered back. "We're settling in."

"You're going to come out to the house for lunch when the service is over."

It wasn't a question, Polly realized. Lacy winked. "I've made my special berry cobbler and Clint has a brisket in the slow cooker as we speak. So it's a done deal. I'll invite some others and we'll have a good ol' time."

Polly nodded, then joined in the singing.

Norma Sue and Esther Mae were in the front row

of the choir, and they were both grinning at her as they sang full out. Esther Mae had on a hat that was overflowing with red poppies. They shook and shimmied with every note she sang.

Smiling at the sight, Polly joined in the singing and promised herself that if she just gave it time one day, she wouldn't feel like the odd person out. One day she'd belong again.

On Wednesday afternoon, Nate found three packages on his porch addressed to Pollyanna. Since she was busy getting the bed-and-breakfast ready, he figured whatever was in the packages might be important, so he loaded them into his truck to drop off on his way past her house. He was hauling cattle to auction in Ranger, and they bawled loudly as he drove.

"Hang on, boys," he said, and turned onto Pollyanna's drive. "Let's see what disaster awaits us." Life at the McDonald house was not boring. That was for certain. Before he even came to a halt, Pollyanna came out onto the porch. She was holding a phone book.

"Hi," she called as he climbed out and grabbed the first package.

"Hi. I've got some packages meant for you. Three of them."

"It's my bedding for the B and B!" she exclaimed, and got so excited she tried to snatch the box from him before he could set in on the porch. They almost bumped heads but missed by a small margin, though his hat tumbled to the ground.

"So, I figure this makes you happy?"

She grimaced, dropped the phone book onto the box and scooped up the hat. "The boxes make me happy. Not attacking your hat. Sorry." She held it out to him.

"Not a problem." Their hands brushed as he took the hat, and he felt a hum of electricity. Unsettled by it, he pulled back and stuck the hat on his head. "There's two more. I'll get them." He strode back down the path, but she followed. "You must really need this stuff," he said.

"I do. But right now I need a vet more. I was just looking up phone numbers when I saw you drive up."

"What's wrong?" he handed her a box, careful not to touch her, and took one himself. The cows knocked around in the trailer and Pollyanna jumped, then laughed nervously. "Sorry, the boys are a rowdy bunch," he said, moving away from her and heading to the house. He needed to get on the road.

"One of Bogie's stitches is puffy and I wanted to take him into the nearest vet and get him checked out. I should have already found one around here, but I haven't had the chance. I'm thinking he might need a round of antibiotics or something."

He opened the screen door and set the boxes down one at a time inside. Pollyanna had picked up the phone book and was studying it. Nate glanced at the trailerload of cattle and back at her. "I could take you into Ranger. The vet's office is just down the street from where I'm headed."

"Oh, I couldn't ask you to do that. Just give me his name and I'll take care of it. I have to pick Gil up today anyway. Max had a dentist appointment, so Rose picked him up early."

Miss Independent. He wasn't too happy about the impromptu invitation he'd tossed out there, either. For more than one reason. First, he still wasn't comfortable spending time around Pollyanna, and second, the vet was a she. A single she he'd been avoiding as much as possible because she was more interested in him than his animals. Pollyanna was giving him an out.

One he didn't feel any more comfortable taking.

"We can swing by and pick Gil up. It won't take me long to unload the cows. We can call the vet from the truck." He wasn't sure what he was getting himself into, but he couldn't ignore that Pollyanna and Gil needed his help. He thought about dinner the other night. "Besides," he added, "Gil told me you were wanting to buy a goat. The parents of the receptionist at the vet's office raise them. I'm sure she'd be glad to fix you up. We could probably even swing by and bring it back in the trailer today." He glanced at her car sitting in the drive. "I don't think a goat will fit in that matchbox." He grinned. "So, what'll it be?"

She made a cute face at the car remark, but didn't answer right away. He waited while she thought about it.

"Gil really wants a goat," she said at last. "So if you're game, we're in."

"I'm game." A little reluctant, but game.

Within a few moments they were heading toward

the school with Bogie sitting on the seat behind them. His left eyelid was swollen slightly. Looking at it, Nate didn't think it was too bad, but he had a feeling Pollyanna didn't take chances with the health of those in her care. Regardless of species.

Nate had thought about Gil and that bird often over the past few days. And truth was he kept thinking about the dinner they'd shared that night, too. It had felt good sitting around Pollyanna's table listening to Gil talk about his bird. Watching them interact together.

And Pollyanna McDonald could cook. No, she could *more* than cook. For a man whose mealtime for the past three years had been spent leaning against the kitchen counter beside the microwave eating whatever it was that he'd just zapped or poured out of a can, a home-cooked meal was a treat. But even being that starved for a good meal, he'd recognized greatness when he'd tasted it. He'd practically made a pig out of himself sitting at her table. He hadn't been able to help it. She'd watched him with a mixture of amazement and mirth. He had a funny notion that she understood.

"This gives me a way to say thank you for that home-cooked meal you treated me to the other night." Boy, was that an understatement.

"That meal was my thank-you for all you've done for me since I arrived." She paused, her hands clasped in her lap. "I'll owe you another one after this."

Nate liked the idea of that more than he was comfortable admitting. He told himself it was because of the meal. What man wouldn't do what he could to have a meal like that again? Nate might not be the happiest cowboy on the planet, but he wasn't a fool.

For the next few miles, an uneasy silence surrounded them. He found himself tossing around several conversations, but rejected them all.

"When word gets out about your cooking, your bed-and-breakfast is going to be so booked you're not going to have time to breathe. How do you plan to work that?" he asked at last.

"Work it?" She tilted her head and looked at him quizzically.

"Yeah, the business, Gil, the animals you're wanting to get. Are you going to hire someone to help you?"

"I'll eventually hire some help."

"You might need to do it sooner than you think." He knew the minute he said it that she didn't appreciate his comment. Her green eyes flashed fire and her shoulders stiffened. Nate chastised himself. If she was tying herself down too tightly to the place, that was her business and he should have kept his mouth shut. "Look, I don't know where that came from. What you do isn't any of my business. I'm sorry."

She met his gaze and her expression softened. "No, I overreacted. I can take care of it at first, I'm thinking, and can hire help if needed. Rose can pick Gil up from school for me when I need her to. It would be a great blessing if I did need help immediately."

The school came into view up ahead. Nate hadn't meant to sound discouraging. He thought she'd do well. "It could certainly happen. I've never seen anything like the way people flood into town for one of the festivals the ladies put on. Miss Adela is always turning people away at her place. Even with having moved out to Sam's and having the extra room to put another weekender up, she's still turning them away. At least, that's what I heard."

"That's what she told me back when I was deciding if this was a viable place to move. Still, the summer and weekends will be busiest. Because of that, I feel like I can give Gil the attention he deserves."

She paused, and Nate glanced back to see she was biting her lip, seemingly worrying about something. "You've thought it all out. Sounds good." He had a strong need to encourage her.

She sighed. "I need to support myself and Gil. Gil is my first priority. He's lost one parent. He certainly doesn't need to feel like his mom is too busy, but I have to do this for us. I don't really have a choice."

She folded her hands in her lap. Her knuckles were white. It struck him that she sounded as if she was trying to convince herself.

"You're doing what you need to do," he said. "God's going to take care of you. Have you always worried this much?" he added, because he was curious—despite not wanting to be.

"Marc. He always said I was a born worrywart. I…" She hesitated and Nate glanced at her as he pulled into the school parking lot. "I hate it, actually. But I can't seem to help it. There is so much…" Her voice trailed off and she turned her face to the window.

Nate reached out and tugged gently on a strand of her curly hair. "You're doing good, Pollyanna."

She glanced back at him and gave a small smile, but it didn't quite meet her eyes. "I hope so. I really hope so."

Nate didn't know what to say. He could only imagine the weight she must be feeling.

He wondered how she was financially. She'd said she needed to support herself and Gil. But how bad was it? Not that it was any of his business. She didn't look as if she were in a bind. That big Victorian hadn't been cheap, and she'd had professional movers move her in. Still, appearances could be deceiving. He hoped for her sake and Gil's that her husband had had the good sense to look out for their best interests in case of his death.

Nate slowed the truck. He'd always been a hard worker, and Kayla had teased him about being a miser. But even with that, he'd made certain to have a life-insurance plan in place that would have provided for Kayla and their children, if they'd had any, in the event of his death. The way he looked at it, a man's duty to provide for his family held whether he was alive or dead.

Of course, that was just him. He hoped for Gil and Pollyanna that Marc had felt the same way. But if that were so, it didn't stand to reason that she'd be so worried.

He reined in his thoughts, telling himself again that this wasn't his business. Pollyanna was his neighbor, and he was helping her out. But that was where her business and his business ended.

His hero. The thought sent an uneasy tremor through Polly as she listened to Gil and Nate talk. She had to admit she liked the way Nate interacted with Gil. No wonder Gil had exploded with excitement upon seeing Nate.

The man had gotten more than he'd bargained for when they'd moved in next door to him.

She was still surprised by him. After their first meeting she'd never have imagined. Well, she'd never have imagined that he was as caring as he was. She had to admit that deep down there was a niggling bit of sorrow when Gil looked up at him. Sorrow that it wasn't his daddy he was looking up at so adoringly. She told herself it was a reasonable thing for her to feel, and then set it in the corner of her heart.

She found herself wondering about Nate's wife. What type of woman would Nate Talbert love? Of course, it was none of her business. Still, that didn't stop the idea from popping into her head. He must have loved his wife very much. She knew he missed her. It was obvious that he still had hard moments, as she did. It had eased with time, but sometimes, the familiar pain returned…and she welcomed it. It proved that Marc had meant the world to her. That he'd been here. That he wasn't forgotten.

She wondered if Nate felt that way.

She watched Gil as she talked. He missed his daddy, but seemed to be adjusting and moving forward. Like she wanted him to do. But he still hurt. It was there in his actions, in the earnest way he looked at other boys and their fathers.

Polly frowned thinking about that. This swift and total infatuation with Nate could be dangerous.

She knew she could never replace Marc in her life and she had no desire to. But Gil was a different story. It was natural for a boy to seek out someone to look up to. And of course, with Nate basically riding to their rescue at every turn, it was only natural. But... *But what?*

Her son had been hurt enough, that was what. And by the looks of it, so had Nate. So, she argued with herself, this was a positive thing. They might be good for each other.

She bit her lip and wiped her suddenly damp palm on her jeans. What if at some point Nate decided that a kid trailing around after him wasn't ideal? Or that the widow and her kid living next door to him were more of a bother than he cared to deal with?

What happened if Gil got attached and then Nate pulled back?

You can't protect Gil from everything, Polly.

Marc's words rang in her head. She knew it was true. At least her mind knew it was true, it was her heart that needed to get the message.

Listening to Gil, she knew it was too late to pull him back from this new friendship. All she could do was pray that God would meet his needs and show her how to be both mother and father to him. And that God would continue to put people like Nate into his life who would supply things she couldn't give him. She clung to the verse, *I will never leave you or forsake you.* God had been good to them. It would have been better if He'd let Gil have his father by his side all of his childhood. But that hadn't been in the greater plan.

Nate laughed at something Gil said, drawing her back from her thoughts and prayers. Looking at him now, she wondered for the first time what it would have been like to lose Marc and have nothing of him to hold on to. Gil was her life. Her reason for making the progress she'd made… Her heart ached with just the thought of not having him to carry on a part of Marc. She thanked God every day that he'd been spared.

Her heart ached for Nate. She wondered if he'd wanted children. God had been good to her, in so many ways. But Gil. Gil was the biggest blessing of all and gave her reason to keep going.

She wondered what kept Nate going.

Chapter Seven

They dropped the trailer load of bawling cows off at the auction. It was after five before they headed toward the vet who'd agreed to see Bogie after she'd finished with her other appointments. When they finished there, they were going to swing by and pick up a baby goat.

"So you're sure you want a goat?" Nate asked after he'd driven the truck back out onto the road.

Polly heard the skepticism in his voice. For more than one reason, she thought. "Yes. Like I said the other night, I also want a cow I can name Betsy and plenty of chickens. My last name *is* McDonald." She smiled, feeling relaxed, despite her earlier worries. Marc had always teased her that she had the heart of "Old McDonald" and needed to live in the country. "I want to give my boarders the whole country effect. Fresh eggs and fresh milk and cream from a cow. Of course, I'll need to learn—"

"I'm not drinkin' no milk out-uv-a cow!" Gil grunted

from the backseat. He had his arm around Bogie and his expression was as full of disgust as his voice.

Nate chuckled. "It all comes out of a cow, pardner."

"Ugh. I'll pretend it didn't. I mean, I want a cow and a baby calf. But I really want a goat. I heard they eat *anything*. Back home, Bobby Jackson said his grandpa's goat ate a tire. A whole tire!"

"That would be pretty neat." Nate met Polly's gaze with a slight smile. Polly's stomach tilted.

He drove into the parking lot of the vet clinic and parked in front of the brick building. Nate held the door open for them as they all entered. Polly was brushing past him when she bumped into Bogie. She would have gone down if Nate hadn't reached out and grasp her elbow.

"Whoa, there," he said gently.

Looking up, Polly's legs felt boneless. "Thank you," she managed to say.

"Nate, how in the world are you?"

The squeal drew Polly's attention to the woman sitting behind the desk. She was in her mid to late fifties and she was holding both hands outstretched, a diet soda in one hand and a pen with a flower stuck on the end of it in the other. She slammed the can down on the counter and rammed the flowering pen behind her ear as she came around the counter and gave Nate a hug. Nate's expression was comical as he found himself with his arms trapped against his side while being lifted off the floor by the rail-thin woman.

"Ain't he just the cutest thing you ever saw?" she said, setting him down. Grinning, she goosed him in the sides before turning to Polly. Nate was as pink as Pollyanna's great aunt Merna's rouge!

The brazen woman winked and scrunched her face. "That's a perk of my job, getting to hug all the cute cowboys. Gotta tell you, though, this one here…" She clucked her tongue as she zipped back around the counter. "He's special. It was a shame when the good Lord left him a widower. Just don't know what He's thinking sometimes."

The words, so plainspoken, might have been almost irreverent, except that there was kindness in her eyes and Polly saw that it was evident that Beth, as Nate introduced her, just spoke what was in her heart. Polly liked her instantly, no tiptoeing around for this one.

"It's nice to see things moving forward," Beth continued, looking from Pollyanna to Nate, her meaning obvious. Okay *some* tiptoeing might be nice, Polly thought as her gaze shot to Nate. She knew her consternation mirrored his own.

"Nate says you can get me a goat," Gil piped up, drawing Beth's attention.

Polly breathed a sigh of relief at the sudden subject shift.

"Like I told Nate when he called, my parents would love to *give* you a goat," Beth said. "They're actually getting out of the business because they want to travel more and the goats tie them down too much."

"We need a goat that likes to eat," Gil said, scooting up to the counter. "One that likes tires. They got one of them?"

Beth chuckled, the silk flower tucked at her ear

jiggling. "Well, honey, this is your lucky day. I know just the goat for you. I'll call them right now."

Polly was smiling at Gil when the door from the examining room opened and a striking woman with a glistening blond ponytail stepped into the waiting room. It was probably Polly's imagination, but she thought Nate took a step behind her as the woman settled amazing eyes on him. Amazing eyes that, Polly realized with interest, were looking at Nate as if he were a Hershey Bar.

"Hello, Nate," she drawled in a silky southern voice. "I haven't seen you in ages."

So that was how it was, Pollyanna thought, glancing at Nate. Maybe he wasn't as reclusive as everyone thought.

Nate took one look at the you-never-called-me-but-the-offer-still-stands smile of Susan's and wanted to turn tail and run for the hills. He sure hoped Pollyanna didn't notice he'd stepped closer to her. He'd actually forgotten about Susan for a few minutes, he'd been so busy talking to Gil. If it hadn't been for having seen Gil's devastation at the prospect of losing Pepper, and feeling a need to help Pollyanna, he wouldn't be standing here in the first place.

He'd been using this clinic for years, but Doc Riggs had retired a little over a year ago and his practice had been bought by Susan. She was single and had asked him out the first time she'd come out to help him pull a calf. Nate had been uncomfortable around her ever since. It wasn't that she wasn't a nice woman, she seemed to be, it had just shaken him up. Kayla had been dead for only two years when Susan had first asked him out. He hadn't gotten used to the idea that he was a single man, much less that he was date material—he'd still felt like he was a married man. Susan asking him out made him realize that people thought it was time for him to move on.

Move on.

The words still made his stomach roll.

He pushed the thoughts aside and focused.

"Hello," he said as Susan looked from him to Pollyanna, then back again. "I've been keeping pretty busy," he hedged. "This is Pollyanna McDonald." He looked from Susan to Pollyanna.

Speculation laced Pollyanna's eyes and it made him more uncomfortable than before.

"We're Nate's new neighbors," she offered, holding out her hand to shake Susan's.

"And we're gonna look at some goats after you fix Bogie's eye," Gil chimed in.

Susan settled questioning eyes on Nate. He wanted to leave. He didn't want to date anyone and he didn't want anyone getting the wrong idea, either. He reached for Bogie. "If you'll lead the way, I'll carry this big brute in for you," he said taking control of the situation.

He was relieved when Susan turned and led the way into the cramped examination room. Nate held the wiggling dog while Susan moved in too close for comfort to examine him. The dog, that is. But Nate was acutely aware he was still under the microscope himself. The examination only took a few minutes, but they were some of the most uncomfortable minutes of Nate's life.

"It was nice to meet you, Susan," Pollyanna said as they were leaving with a prescription of antibiotics and the suggestion that Bogie wear the cone another few days.

Nate all but herded Pollyanna and Gil as he pushed them toward the door.

"I'm sure I'll see you again," Pollyanna said, pausing. Nate rammed into her. "I have a regular zoo at my house. Do you work with birds and turtles?"

Susan laughed, leaning against the door frame. "Yes, I do. And goats, too."

Nate nudged Pollyanna. "Thanks. We better be getting to that goat," he said, knowing that would at least get Gil moving.

Susan followed them as far as the porch. "The next time I'm out Mule Hollow way, I might stop by and visit your little farm."

"Oh!" Polly exclaimed, spinning and drawing Nate up short again. "That would be unbelievably nice of you. I'll give you directions—"

"There's no need. If you're Nate's neighbor, I can find you. I'll stop in and say hi to you, too, Nate." She smiled at him, her meaning more than clear. "See y'all later."

Nate nodded. What else could he do? He was certain he was as red as the old work rag balled up on the dashboard of his truck. It was as much from frustration as anything.

"She seems nice," Pollyanna commented when they were finally on the road again.

"Yeah," he grunted, not at all interested in discussing who was nice and who wasn't. When he'd married Kayla he'd married her for life. He'd been off the market the first time he ever saw her. And as far as he was concerned he still was.

With the way Pollyanna looked, he was more than confident she'd had her fair share of attention since her husband's death.

He wondered how she felt about the subject.

Chapter Eight

"Bert! No, Bert!"

At the sound of Gil's excited screams, Polly dropped her paint roller and raced to the open doorway. Her heart was pounding as she ran down the steps and around the side of the house. Two days ago they'd gone to buy a baby goat and instead they'd come home with Bert. Bert was a crotchety old billy goat, older than dirt. She'd tried to talk Gil into picking out a baby goat, but the moment he'd heard Bert's story he'd wanted the old goat. Since the older couple was getting out of the goat business, they said no one wanted Bert because he was old and ornery. Gil had said the baby goats would get homes, but that they had to take Bert so he would have a place to live. And so it was that Bert had come to live with them. He'd immediately started following Gil around like a puppy, nibbling at him as if he were a cookie. And Bogie was being terrorized. Bert loved trying to eat his collar.

It hadn't taken her long to realize that between Bert and Gil, she was going to pass gray and go straight to white hair. Just yesterday she'd caught both of them standing on top of the feed shed. How either of them got there she couldn't exactly say. The only good thing was that the shed was only about twelve feet off the ground. Compared to three stories, it seemed somewhat tame in perspective. Still, as she raced around the house, she wasn't sure what to expect.

It wasn't until she'd reached the side yard that she realized Gil's squeals were from laughing.

Bert had knocked Gil down, had latched on to a button on his shirt and was trying to eat it.

Polly rushed forward, grabbed the goat's collar and tried to pull him away from Gil. "Let go, Bert. Let go*oo*." Bert wasn't giving up the button and Gil wasn't helping, since he was too busy giggling to save himself. And why would she expect anything different? He *had* wanted a goat that would eat tires! Polly was out of breath when she finished wrestling with the now-calm goat. He'd gotten his prize during the scuffle, and stood happily chewing the button, watching her with black eyes from beneath his bushy eyebrows. His white goatee moved up and down with the rhythm of his jaw, making him resemble Applegate Thornton, one of the older men who sat up at Sam's Diner playing checkers every morning.

Polly was beginning to wonder at the wisdom of wanting a goat in the first place. He'd started eating her bushes the instant they'd unloaded him. He tried to eat anything he could get his mouth around. She'd had to guard her tulips constantly. Nate had warned her that an old goat might be more than she was bargaining for, but she'd chosen not to take his advice.

The man was big on advice.

"Gil, honey, how did he get out of his pen?" The animal obviously couldn't be contained. He always got out.

"I don't know. I think he ate the latch."

Polly wouldn't doubt that for a minute. She stomped to the back of the house to the gate beside the shed. Sure enough, the rope that had been tied to the metal gate and latched to the nail on the post was gone.

She looked around for it on the ground, but it was nowhere. "Did you take the rope, Gil?"

"Nope. Bert musta ate it. If he'll eat Bogie's collar and my buttons he'll eat a rope. 'Cause it can't fight back."

"You've got a point, kiddo. How did he get you on the ground back there?"

"When I was bent over tying my shoestrings he snuck up on me and butted me with his head and sent me flying. Man, it was awesome. I hit the ground and rolled like a *hundred times* before I stopped. My head was spinning—"

"Are you okay?" Polly gasped, fearing she'd made a bad judgment.

"Are you kidding? It was *awesome!*"

Boys. "Come on, let's go find something else to use as a latch."

"Yeah, something Bert can't eat," Gil said, following her into the small shed. "Mom, do you like Nate?"

Startled, Polly paused digging through a bin of odds and ends. "Well, sure I do. He's a good neighbor."

Gil kicked a can and stuffed his hands in his pockets. "I think that woman vet did, too. Did you see the gooey way she was looking at him?"

Who wouldn't have? She'd also noticed that she was using Polly as an excuse to drop by his place for a visit. But it wasn't any of her business. She just wondered if Susan noticed how uneasy her attentions made Nate? It hadn't taken Polly but a moment to realize that if it hadn't been for them he'd have run.

"There's a chain," Gil yelped, efficiently bringing Polly's thoughts back to the moment.

Looking up to where he was pointing, she spotted the chain coiled on the top shelf. "Yep, that's a chain, all right. But now I need a ladder to get to it and a ladder I don't have."

"There's a bucket back here," Gil exclaimed, disappearing out the door.

Polly hurried after him to the end of the shed where he was tugging a five-gallon feed bucket out of a tangle of honeysuckle growing over the fence and up the side of the shed. Bert hadn't gotten to it yet, but Polly had no doubts he'd take care of it soon enough.

"That'll work great." Taking it from him, she headed back inside.

"It's a good thing I found it before Bert did or he'd eat it." Gil laughed. "I'm gonna go make sure he's not eatin' poor ole Bogie."

"That might be a good idea. And please keep him away from my tulips," she called, setting the bucket down and stepping onto it. Wobbling, she grasped the lower shelf to steady herself, then stretched up for the chain.

And that's when she saw the snake! *A big black snake.*

A scream lodged in Polly's throat as she toppled off the bucket to her knees, her heart thundering like a burst of dynamite. Scrambling up, she stumbled out the door faster than a speeding…faster than a— Well, she was too scared to think of what she was running faster than, but she was certain if someone had been watching they'd find her evacuation of the shed spectacularly entertaining on several different levels.

A hero she most definitely wasn't when it came to snakes. She didn't stop moving until she was almost to the house. Logic told her she'd probably scared the snake as badly as it had scared her. Only problem was, she didn't care. It could have her shed! Just thinking about its beady little eyes made her recoil.

What now?

Polly paced back and forth. She knew the answer. She didn't like the answer, but she knew she had to dig deep and somehow find the courage to go back in there and reclaim her territory.

It was probably just a chicken snake. Like that mattered to her! Snakes—chicken, grass or nasty—gave her the creeps.

She paced some more. Marc had always dealt with the awful creatures. "Don't you laugh," she scolded out loud. Marc's memory was suddenly so alive, as if he were standing beside her chuckling in his playful baritone. He'd had a great sense of humor—not that this was funny. But if he were here he'd be laughing while watching her work up the gumption to go back and attack.

He'd called her tenacity for overcoming obstacles her gumption. And he'd loved it. He never knew that most of the time it was his strength that had fueled hers. With him by her side, she'd felt as if she could do anything.

Halting, Polly stared at the shed. Since Marc's death there had been so many things she'd had to learn to do alone. Talking to him gave her courage. "I can do this."

Sure you can.

Like so many other times when she'd thought she couldn't do something, she could almost hear his voice speaking from her heart giving her courage…and making her ache with missing him. She straightened her shoulders.

"Sure I can," she muttered. "I can climb this mountain, too." And she could. Then she thought about the broken water valve and hesitated. For just a moment. "You will do this," she demanded. If anyone were watching they'd think she'd lost her marbles. Looking up toward a clear blue heaven, she frowned. "But, just so you know. I'm never going to speak to you again if I have a heart attack and die trying to get rid of that snake." That said, she sucked in a deep breath and stomped forward.

There was a hoe leaning against the side of the shed, and she grabbed it with trembling fingers. "Mr. Snake, you're going down."

Her steps tentative, she lifted the hoe, banged it on the side of the shed and waited a moment. She tapped it again for good measure before finally sticking her head inside the open doorway. She shuddered and her heart thumped out the theme song to *Jaws* as she stepped inside....

"Is something wrong?"

"Whaaat!" Polly screamed, spinning around, hoe ready for war. Nate Talbert! The big bazooka was standing in the doorway right behind her. Blocking her exit!

"Whoa, careful with that thing. I didn't mean to startle you," he said, holding his hands up like a shield.

"Didn't your mother teach you not to sneak up on people?" Polly snapped, pushing past him and storming out into the open yard. "You scared the daylights out of me." As if he couldn't tell.

"Sorry," he said, following her. Stopping in front of her, his hands on his hips, his booted feet planted shoulder width apart, he studied her. And she...she studied him right back, the bum! The very idea, sneaking up on her like that...looking all strong and appealing—she corrected that thought—capable. He looked capable! Lightbulb moment! *He* could kill a snake. Or catch it, or scare it off. Like he'd just done to her.

"It was a snake." She shivered. "I *hate* snakes."

Nate's mouth quirked on the edges, his eyes lit with understanding and he reached for the hoe. "I'll take care of this."

"Hi-ya, Nate," Gil said, coming around the side of the house, Bogie and Bert running behind him. "You found her. I told you she was back here."

Nate smiled. "Yep, I found her in the shed just like you told me—"

"No, Bert!" Gil interrupted when Bert suddenly latched on to Bogie and started tugging. Bogie barked and tried to back away while Gil pulled on Bert and Bert pulled on the mutilated collar.

"Its okay, Bogie," Polly soothed, taking the harassed pup's side as the tug-of-war ensued. Bogie shook his head back and forth frantically, and Bert held on like glue, knocking poor Gil around like a kid on a bucking bull.

"Help!" Polly laughed, looking up toward Nate. He tossed the hoe out of the way and grabbed for Bogie, too. The instant he added his strength to the opposing side, Bert let go. Probably out of sheer meanness. The lack of resistance sent Polly, Nate and Bogie thudding to the ground.

Nate started laughing. She did, too.

"You two okay?" Gil asked, grinning quizzically at them with his hands on his hips.

Polly nodded and met Nate's eyes just as his laughter trailed off and Polly saw his eyes shadow. "Gil," she said gently. "Why don't you take poor Bogie inside. He's been traumatized enough for one afternoon. I'll take care of Bert. You can have some cookies and milk."

"Grrreat!"

She watched him jog off, then glanced at Nate. "Are you okay?"

He stood, his expression grim, his eyes so grief stricken that Polly thought she'd never seen anything so wounded in all of her life. Except she had. She recognized it as the look she saw in her own eyes when she looked in a mirror after something happened to make her miss Marc anew. Grief came in unrelenting, devastating waves like that. Even years later.

Instead of answering, Nate held out a hand to her. Unsteadily, she slipped hers into his and let him tug her up. His eyes remained cheerless as he turned away and strode to the fence. So alone, Polly thought, her heart wrenching as she watched him, his shoulders hunched as he stared out toward the pond below.

Polly wondered for a second if she was just imagining things. What made her think that she could read his mind? She didn't really know Nate. But her heart told her she was right. He was thinking about his wife.

Taking a deep breath, she went to stand beside him. "It's hard, missing them," she said softly.

The only sign that he heard her was the slight nod of his head. Polly respected his response, if he wanted to share he would. She simply wanted him to know she would listen if he needed someone to talk to. Her gaze lingered on his unyielding profile that only moments ago had been alive with laugh lines. She longed to ease his pain.

"Yes," he admitted finally, his voice cracking. His eyes softened for a moment before he brought the shields back up. In silence they watched a couple of birds play a game of carefree chase out over the pond.

"What was her name?" Polly asked softly, curious about the woman he'd obviously loved so much, and realizing that she had yet to ask for that important piece of information.

She felt his smile as his entire countenance shifted beside her. "Kayla."

The way he said his wife's name touched Polly—rolling off his lips in a loving whisper. She could hear his love and was drawn to him, feeling such a connection with him. "Do you ever hear her talk to you?" *Way to go, Pollyanna.* He'd think she was some crazy crackpot who heard voices. And that wasn't it at all.

"No one's ever asked me that before." His voice was low, stunned.

"I'm sorry. I—"

"Yes."

Relief washed over her. She'd thought she'd upset him. "That's a relief, I thought maybe I was the only one." She smiled, unable to completely believe she was teasing about this.

He shrugged, a half smile lifting his lips. "She gets mad that I don't listen to her."

Polly wrapped her arms across her middle and turned to look up at him fully, her shoulder resting against a cedar fence post. She could tell he was shy about sharing something so personal. She understood wholeheartedly. "I know exactly what you mean. My Marc, he pushes me… Not really, you understand. But knowing what he would have said or expected in certain situations helps me." She grunted as a half chuckle escaped. "It's a good thing, though there are some times if he were here I'd wring his neck because of it." She laughed at that, knowing it wasn't true. She'd hug the breath out of him and never let him go. "God has been with me every step of the way, but half of the progress I've made was because of the memory of Marc's voice in my head." She sighed, feeling the soft April wind whisper over her skin, bringing with it the memory of his touch. "It's one of God's gifts, you know." Her voice was troubled even to her own ears. Sometimes it took everything she had inside her heart to keep focused on those gifts and not the aching loss.

Nate turned to her, his dark eyes questioning. "A gift?"

She focused. "Yes. I love having Marc's voice in my head. It's a way of keeping him with me. Losing the sound of his voice is one of the things I fear most. I know that day is coming." Polly thanked God every night for the memories. Though with each passing year she lost things. Little things. The feel of his hand on hers. The sound of his laughter…things he said. He was drifting away from her slowly, piece by piece. Oh, she knew she wouldn't forget everything…but she didn't want to forget anything. Not one second.

It had been two years, though. It was time for her to move forward and let some of the past fade. She sniffed and forced the disheartening thought away. It was inevitable that memories faded over time. She was so thankful for Gil. Period. On his own merit, but also because she could see Marc in him. He looked so much like his dad. People thought he looked like her on first glance because he had her coloring, but he looked like his dad. He laughed like him, held his head like Marc when he was thinking. He tied his shoestrings backward like his dad had taught him, along with the totally weird way he held his fork. She was comforted knowing that even if some memories faded, she had Gil to keep others alive.

Nate didn't have that.

"So what does Kayla get mad at you about?"

He held her gaze for the longest time, as if deciding if he wanted to share something so personal. But Polly knew that maybe he needed to share with someone. They hadn't known each other long, yet this connected them like nothing else could. She cocked her head to the side and smiled encouragingly up at him, urging him to let her in.

He frowned and took a deep breath and let it out slowly. "That I don't move on."

"And you don't have any desire to move on."

He looped his thumbs through his belt loops. "Honestly, sometimes I wish I did."

"But you don't." It wasn't a question, just an observation. She had the same feeling.

"No, I don't. At least I haven't. How about you?"

"Nope. I feel so blessed to have had what I had with Marc. I can't begin to imagine loving someone else. I mean, I get so lonely sometimes…" She let the thought trail off. "But I can live with that. There are worse things than being lonely. I would much rather be lonely than make a mistake and tarnish something that was so great. Marc was my best friend…."

"Kayla was mine." Nate's gaze softened. "How did Marc die?"

Polly took a deep breath, detaching from the explanation the way she'd learned to do. "A car accident, stopped at a red light. Gil was with him and

I thank God he survived. Without a scratch." The tragic irony of it still got to her. After all the fear and worry over Marc's love of speed—he'd been killed sitting quietly at a red light smiling into the backseat at his son. It had taken her a long time to be able to say those words without tears. And she wasn't always successful even now. "Life can change in the blink of an eye...."

He nodded.

"And Kayla, how did Kayla die?" She hated this, but it needed to be out of the way.

"Slowly," he said. Bitterness marked his expression as he turned away. Polly didn't push, instead she gave him time to take the conversation where he needed.

"Hey," he said suddenly, his tone brightening falsely. "What do you say we go see about that snake?"

"Oh, the snake!" Polly had forgotten all about the snake with all that had gone on since finding it in her shed. But to her surprise she was glad to have the snake as a distraction. "If he's smart, he's gone by now."

Nate started toward the shed, effectively shutting their conversation down. But Polly knew something had changed between them, she saw it in his eyes when he looked at her, a smile at their edges. They were friends. "That snake's probably heard your last name was McDonald and he's in there waiting on you to adopt him."

Polly grunted, "Boy, is he in for a rude awakening."

Chapter Nine

Nate walked out to his back porch and sat down on the porch swing. His thoughts were burdened as he pushed back and forth with one foot. He'd opened up to Pollyanna today. He hadn't talked to anyone like that since Kayla.

And he'd laughed…really laughed. Like the old days. The kind that came from the bottom of his gut and felt good.

Today it hurt like a dam exploding inside his chest, releasing a little of the aching pressure that was always building inside of him. And surprisingly it had felt good. Just like Pollyanna had said.

Studying the sky, he thought about her. Pollyanna. It had been a relief to talk with someone who understood what he'd lost. That explained why he'd opened up to her.

She had guts. She was funny, too, like Kayla had been.

He smiled, remembering how giddy she'd been

when they'd gone into her shed to find the snake gone. She'd proclaimed, "Lucky for him he's escaped to live another day."

And so had he, Nate thought, letting the swing rock forward. So had he.

He felt like he'd turned a corner. He said a prayer that it was true.

The sign said Sam's Diner and Pharmaceuticals. Polly smiled every time she read the small print proclaiming, *Eat at Your Own Peril 6:00 a.m. to 8:00 p.m.* As if it had been added at a later date, *9:00 p.m. on Thursdays* was written at the bottom.

Instead of going inside immediately she studied the town, the colors, the vividness of it all. Down the street the tall house with the many turrets and green roof had been Adela's family home, which she'd turned into six small apartments and left only two rooms open for bed-and-breakfast boarders, three counting Adela's old room. She'd married and moved in with her husband, Sam. It was a lovely building and Polly was going to go down after lunch and have a tour. She kept thinking about what Nate had said: that once she opened she might be busier than she anticipated. That was a good thing. She could hire help and still be able to give Gil plenty of time and be financially independent.

So she was taking a tour of Adela's to see if she could get any pointers, but first she was meeting the ladies for lunch here at the diner. She loved the diner. A person wasn't an official Mule Hollow resident until they'd dined at Sam's.

When she'd gotten the invitation and since it was Saturday she'd expected to bring Gil with her, but then Nate had called and said he'd promised Gil a riding lesson if she gave the go-ahead. She was still smiling at how excited Gil had been as he rode his bike to Nate's.

She hadn't let herself dwell on the small voice of warning. The voice that said she shouldn't let Gil become too attached to their neighbor. She wasn't certain if the warning was for Gil's protection or for Nate's.

Or for her. But they'd already jumped into the river going downstream and there were no exits. She was just going to have to ride it out and pray that the Lord worked it all out.

So, glad to have the opportunity for a bike ride herself, she'd ridden to town and was feeling more at ease than she'd felt in a very long time. Almost blissful. She loved a good bike ride and had to convince three truckloads of cowboys along the way that she didn't need a lift into town. Hitchhikers would be in high cotton around Mule Hollow. Fact was, she and Marc had loved riding and had spent many summer vacations exploring on bikes. It was as tame a sport as Marc endured, and he'd taken it up because she'd refused to ride a motorcycle. Bikes had worked out much better for the family, and since the ripe old age of one, Gil had been as comfortable in a baby bike seat as a car seat.

She had a feeling she was about to lose him, though. The boy was so infatuated with horses. And that was fine with her, she wanted him to have hopes and

dreams of his own, hobbies that made him happy—
though she couldn't help praying that dirt bikes didn't
catch his interest.

She was determined not to cling. She wanted him
to choose his own interests, and animals were a healthy
way to get him to love the outdoors. Mule Hollow
was going to be good for him. Much better than the
congestion of Dallas.

Stepping into the diner, she let herself concentrate on
enjoying herself. Back in the city, there were so many
restaurants that were built new to look old and charming. Fake. Sam's was one-hundred-percent authentic
and nostalgic. The smell of oiled pine and scrumptious
food greeted her and made her mouth water. She
breathed in the scents—hamburgers, bacon—no doubt
left over from a brisk breakfast run. She could smell
Mexican food mingled in the mix, too. Her stomach
growled.

A table of cowboys sitting in one corner tipped
their heads at her as she entered. Recognizing them as
some of the guys who'd offered to give her a lift, she
smiled and said hello.

At the window table, Applegate Thornton and
Stanley Orr sat huddled over a game of checkers. The
first time she'd come to the diner, she'd known from
reading Molly Jacobs's weekly newspaper column
who the two older gentlemen were. They were just as
crotchety in person as the syndicated columnist por-
trayed them. It wasn't every town that had a reporter
bringing it to life across the country each week. But
Mule Hollow did and all because of an ad campaign

to bring women to town to marry the cowboys. It was this unique twist that was bringing weekend traffic to the town. These checker players were part of the charm. They looked up and she smiled.

"You wanna play checkers?" the thin one, Applegate, asked, talking louder than necessary.

She shook her head. "No, sir, you go right ahead. Don't let me interrupt." She raised her voice a notch, hoping he heard her okay.

"He's only askin' ya 'cause I'm whuppin' the pants off of him," Stanley, the slightly plump one, said with a wink.

"What'd you say?" Applegate demanded loudly.

"Oh, you old coot, you ain't foolin' me. I know you heard me. Yor hearin' aid is working fine. Same as mine."

Frowning, Applegate spit a sunflower seed into the spittoon. "Cain't holt it against a man fer tryin' ta hang on to a lead."

"A lead! In yor dreams."

Polly laughed. They were adorable, reminding her of her grandpa and his brothers when they got together.

"Over here, Pollyanna," Esther Mae called from a booth near the back, drawing her attention away from the feuding friends. Polly passed the jukebox on her way and, reaching into her pocket, pulled out a nickel. The jukebox only took a nickel and one never knew what song it would be stuck on.

From the corner Esther Mae exclaimed, "Not the jukebox!"

Polly frowned. "I can't come in here without

putting at least one nickel in." She let the coin drop into the slot and pushed the number for an old Johnny Cash song, her daddy's favorite. As she walked to the table the jukebox whirred to life. Polly laughed as Elvis's silken croon filled the room.

"Here we go," Esther Mae groaned. "I love Elvis as much as the next guy, but if I have to hear him asking me to love him tender one more time I'll scream. I'll show him tender, I'll get me a bat and—"

"Esther Mae," Norma Sue barked. "Get a hold of yourself."

Esther Mae smiled sheepishly as she smoothed her napkin. "Forgive me. But somebody needs to fix that thing."

"Sorry," Polly said. "How long has the jukebox been stuck on that song?"

"Three weeks," Norma Sue said. "She'll live. So how was the ride in? Applegate saw you ride up on a bike." Norma Sue scooted over to allow Polly room to sit down beside her. Adela and Esther Mae smiled from across the table. Elvis sang on.

"It was fantastic. Just what I needed to keep me sane. I think the cattle were curious about me, though. They kept looking at me as if I was riding the oddest horse they'd ever seen."

"Can't say we have too many bike riders in these parts," Esther Mae said, shaking a packet of sweetener. "We're a little too far off the beaten track to even get the occasional long-distance rider and that's a shame, too. I think they look so cute in all their colorful outfits. I was thinking about getting me a pink one."

"Please, deliver us from that," Norma Sue groaned. "Polly, we're glad you're here, but Esther Mae, stay away from biker shorts."

"I was just joking," the redhead snorted, scowling at her friend.

"I hope so. You'd look like a sausage."

Polly fought a smile. "I'm staying away from biker shorts myself. But, you'll see me riding. I try to ride a few times a week. It's just with getting settled and everything I've hardly had a chance." Her attention went to Sam, a small man with a quick, bowlegged step. He burst through the kitchen double doors, looking like a man with a purpose. He wore a white apron, jeans, boots and a long-sleeved shirt. His eyes danced with alertness as he held out his hand.

"Well, hello thar, Pollyanna." She'd met him when she and Gil had first arrived. He looked lovingly over at his wife, Adela, as he latched on to Polly's hand. "I was a wonderin' when you was gonna get back in here."

Polly was trying to focus, but it was hard because though Sam was small, he had an iron grip. Was that bone grinding? She feared her fingers would fall off when, just in the nick of time, he let go.

"I've just been really busy," she managed to say, fighting off a gasp of relief. Beneath the table she flexed her fingers. They still worked.

"Oh, but, dear," Adela chimed in, "we would love to help you more."

"No. You have all done more than enough. Thank you, though. I'm just adding a bit of color to the walls now. I love to paint. I'm giving each room a special technique. Besides, you all did more than enough last week. I can't thank you enough."

She planned to pick up paint next week, but first she had yard work to do. Dirt had been delivered the evening before, and she wanted to get her new flower beds started that evening. When she picked up paint, she planned to pick out plants, too.

"Do y'all like to work on flower beds?" she asked. *Did they ever!* That was all it took for them to launch into the wonders of digging in the dirt. Within minutes plans were made for them to come out the following week and help her with her landscaping. Polly could not believe how blessed she was to live in such a place.

"You girls goin' ta stop talkin' long enough to order something to eat?" Sam asked a few minutes later.

"I got some enchiladas fresh out of the oven, though I need to warn you that Cassie helped me fix 'em and she ain't ever helped me cook before. That young'un's goin' ta starve that poor Jake ta death."

Esther Mae harrumphed. "If anybody can teach her how to cook, it'd be you, Sam. Where is she, anyway?"

"She's with Dottie and the girls from the shelter getting fitted for her wedding dress and their bridesmaid dresses. I think they're all crammed into Ashby's dress store. She was in here early this morning to help me get ready for my Saturday run, and then she was off to get poked and prodded. Her words, not mine."

Norma Sue explained that they were having Cassie's wedding in a few weeks. Then the conversation rounded back to their order, everyone deciding to try Cassie and Sam's enchiladas.

"So where is that sweet boy of yours?" Esther Mae asked. "He's such a cutie. I love kids. I'm hoping some of these newlyweds decide to give Mule Hollow some babies pretty soon."

"No rush," Norma Sue interjected. "A good marriage is set by a firm foundation between newlyweds. Don't rush them, Esther Mae."

"I'm not. I just want more babies to take care of."

"Soon enough, Esther Mae. So where is your boy, Polly?"

"Nate's giving Gil riding lessons today."

There was no way for Polly to miss the expressions of covert delight that flashed around the table.

"So, speaking of Nate. How's that going?"

"Esther Mae," Adela said softly, but Polly heard a warning in her gentle tone.

"I'm not interfering. I'm just asking if Polly and Nate have, you know, gotten to be friends."

Polly had known when she moved to Mule Hollow that she was going to come up against the matchmakers, and she was prepared. "I think we could be called friends. But, ladies, truly, don't set your sights on me. I'm, well, I was married to the most wonderful man in the world…like I told you already, I couldn't—"

Adela reached across the table and placed her fine-boned hand on Polly's arm. "It's all right, dear. We didn't mean anything. But, like I said, I speak from experience." She glanced up at Sam as he returned with glasses of iced tea. The love in her blue eyes was unmistakable. "You can love again."

Maybe so, Polly thought, but there were other issues at play. She had pictures of Marc hanging on the walls of her house and she couldn't ever imagine taking them down and replacing them with someone else's image. She had Gil to consider, too. He needed to see Marc's pictures, and then there would be grandchildren when Gil grew up and married. If she did remarry, her grandchildren would need to know Marc was their grandfather. Needed to hear stories about him. She needed to keep Marc's memory alive, and if she remarried there would be someone else that her grandchildren would call Granddaddy... Polly had almost as hard a time with that thought as she had with Gil calling another man Daddy.

"Nate's an incredible man. But I'm fine as I am. Really," she said firmly.

Sam brought out their plates at that moment and Polly was relieved. But as everyone bowed their heads to say a prayer of thanksgiving, she thought she saw Esther Mae wink at Norma Sue.

Chapter Ten

Polly shoveled dirt from the wheelbarrow and ignored the ache in her back. She wasn't really a yard person by some people's standards, but she liked big flower beds with low-maintenance plants that promised to bloom from spring until late fall. She'd always been a busy person, and finicky plants just didn't fit into her lifestyle. For now, that philosophy would have to work on the grounds of the bed-and-breakfast. But later, maybe next spring when she had her first year behind her, she would stretch herself and really bring this huge yard to life. She could envision arbors and trailing vines and all sorts of nooks in which guests could sit. It felt good thinking about the possibilities.

At the moment she was working on a round bed out in the center of the front yard, where she was going to place a birdbath and surround it with flowers. For now, she was just preparing the soil. Next week she'd actually do the plantings. And she was going to have plenty of advice from the ladies when they came to help. From listening to them, she could tell they knew all the plants that worked best in Mule Hollow's dry climate. They'd also mentioned they were all going to bring her some things from their own yards. She was really looking forward to that.

"Hey, Mom!"

After his riding lesson, Gil had called to see if he could check cows with Nate. She was startled to see the two of them walking from the backyard.

"We rode Taco to check the cows out there." He waved his hand, indicating the pastures that stretched behind the house. Polly's two acres were surrounded by land owned by Nate. There weren't any cattle in the pasture next to the house. They were out there, somewhere beyond the trees.

"It was getting late and Gil was hungry, so I thought I'd drop him off and bring his bike over tomorrow."

"That's great." Polly swiped at her nose, suddenly feeling self-conscious. She probably had dirt all over her face. A glance down at her tank top and shorts confirmed she wasn't filthy, but close to it.

"You need any help?" Nate looked from her to the dirt she was spreading out.

"No. I'm fine. So did you have fun?" she asked Gil.

"Yup. Nate says I can help with a roundup one of these days."

"Oh, did he now?" She cut her eyes sharply at Nate.

Nate put his hands on his hips and looked at her reassuringly. "Not until he's ready. But you have a natural-born horseman on your hands."

She'd overreacted, and she gave him a smile of apology. "Sorry. He is a natural athlete."

"It's okay. Looks like he takes after you."

Polly shook her head. "Marc was the real athletic talent in the family. I just like to ride bikes."

"I'm a chip off the old block," Gil piped in. "That's what Grandpa McDonald says. He's got bunches of pictures and trophies of my dad's. He says all mine are going to go on the shelf right beside them."

"You keep working and you'll be able to add some horsemanship trophies and ribbons to the mix."

"Awesome."

From inside the house, a mournful wail came. Polly hadn't let Bogie out while she was working because she didn't want him getting underfoot. "Why don't you go clean up and eat a sandwich? I'm going to work a little longer."

She felt a little guilty about the sandwich for supper, but today had been a busy day.

Nate reached for her shovel. "Why don't you go take care of him and I'll finish unloading this dirt?"

Polly pulled the shovel out of his reach. "Oh, no. I can do it. Besides, Gil loves to create his own sandwiches. I keep the refrigerator stocked for him."

Nate grinned at her. "You are a stubborn woman, Pollyanna McDonald."

Her grip tightened on the shovel handle. She felt a little foolish refusing his help, especially when he was smiling like that. "I can do this."

"I didn't say you couldn't. I said I wanted to help."

"You want me to bring you a soda when I come back, Nate?" Gil asked. He was grinning, too.

"Sure. If your mom says I can stay."

Polly looked from one to the other and gave up. "Fine. But get your own tool."

Nate chuckled. "I'll be right back."

Polly watched him stride toward the back of the house like a man on a mission. He'd been in her shed and knew where the assortment of garden tools was.

When he returned, he went to work beside her, shoveling and spreading the dirt. "So, what do you have planned for out here?"

Polly paused to shove hair out of her face with the back of her hand. The wayward strand immediately fell exactly where it had been tickling her damp cheek. It was nearing six o'clock, so it wasn't as hot as it had been, but she knew her face was probably pink from exertion beneath the dusting of grime. Ignoring her vanity, she met his gaze. "Well, for this year, something as maintenance free as I can get it." She told him what she had planned and mentioned all the ladies coming out next week.

"Now, that should be interesting," he said as he handed her his shovel. He grabbed the handles of the empty wheelbarrow and headed toward the dirt pile across the driveway.

"They're really a lively lot," she said.

That got her an amused glance. "Now, *that's* an understatement." They both grinned at the truth of his comment. "But they've done wonders for Mule Hollow with all their wacky matchmaking schemes, town festivals and theater productions. No telling what they're going to come up with next. I'd believe anything, though, because I never thought I'd see the day that a bunch of cowpokes would stand up on a stage and sing."

"Have they tried fixing you up yet?" She watched his expression carefully. She wondered if he suspected that they were trying to now. She also was wondering why on earth she'd brought this up when she was already uncomfortable enough.

His lips flattened and his knuckles whitened on the handles of the wheelbarrow. "I'd think they'd have to be pretty desperate to set their sights on me. Pollyanna—"

"You can call me Polly. It's a lot shorter." Why had she said that?

They'd reached the dirt and he'd parked the wheelbarrow now. He took his shovel and settled thoughtful eyes on her. Her heart skidded at the intensity. "I like Pollyanna," he said gently. "It suits you."

Polly's nerves frazzled further and the laugh that escaped her rode on the wings of attraction. The very idea took the wind from her. "And how's that?" she managed to say, trying to hide her discomfort.

"You make people smile."

His comment totally took her by surprise. Especially since his expression had changed in an instant and was far from smiling. It made her think he'd just as soon she dropped off the face of the earth when he turned away and plunged his shovel into the dirt with all the force of sledgehammer.

"You don't have to act so happy about that," she

said. He slid his gaze toward her as he dumped the dirt into the wheelbarrow.

"I bet before your husband died, you really made people smile."

"If you're asking if I was different before Marc died, the answer is yes." She studied Nate's profile.

"So was I."

There it was again. The connection. Polly looked away and started working. He did, too. They were two people trying to find their way. Her chest felt tight with emotion.

"Did you get angry?" he asked after a minute.

"Honestly, no. At least not in the sense you're asking. Everyone told me I should expect it, that I would and that it was a normal progression toward healing. But I didn't." The tightness in her chest had eased some. She paused, suddenly wanting to talk. She turned back to face him, glancing at Gil. "There were times when I could feel anger trying to build up inside me. But when that started I reminded myself again of how blessed I'd been and still was to have loved Marc at all."

Nate held her gaze as he handed her back the shovel. It did things to her insides. Polly took a deep breath to settle her stomach. "God gave me so many blessings. First he gave me a remarkable life with the love of my life. And then he gave me Gil. How could I be mad at God about that?"

Nate lay his hand on Polly's arm. "Can we continue this later?"

She looked at his hand as a mixture of emotions swirled inside her. "Okay." She blinked, meeting his gaze and feeling as shaky inside as the smile she gave him. He squeezed her arm and his touch almost scorched her skin, or at least it felt that way. Polly swallowed hard and felt more than a little disturbed by her reaction. Nate turned away and reached for the wheelbarrow just as Gil slid to a halt beside him.

"I got food in my belly so I'm good to go. Can I push that thing?" He held out a grape soda to Nate.

"Hang on to that for me." Nate chuckled and glanced over his shoulder at Polly, clearly totally unaffected by the touch, she thought. "When we get over there you can help. I loaded this up with almost more than I can handle."

"Okay," Gil said, trotting beside Nate, as happy as Polly had ever seen him.

"I may just have to give the young man a job. What do you think about that?"

"A job!" Gil exclaimed. "Woo-hoo! Can I muck out some more stalls?"

"Only Gil would find cleaning out horse stalls fun," Polly commented.

Nate grinned, and Polly shook herself mentally to shift focus to him and her son. It was one thing for him to offer an occasional afternoon. But a job?

"Only if I can pay you, though."

"You mean with *money?*"

"Well, sure, pardner. I'm not going to have you work that hard for nothing. A man needs to be paid for his work."

Standing beside the flower bed, Polly felt her heart do a spin. Gil's eyes grew twice their normal size.

"Wow," he said. "Did you hear that, Mom?"

"I heard. But really, Nate, it's not necessary." She hated seeing Gil frown but it was true. She didn't want Nate thinking he was obligated to have Gil underfoot just because they were neighbors.

"For you, maybe, but I could use some afternoon help every now and again."

Gil's smiled bloomed again. Polly bit her lip and held Nate's gaze. The man was impossible. "Okay, then. But you will not pay him."

"I certainly will."

"I pay him an allowance for the chores he does around the house. He doesn't need your money."

"These aren't chores. This is a job, and a man can always use a little extra cash."

Polly didn't really appreciate his bucking her on this issue. Gil was her son. She looked at Gil and he was almost pleading with her with his eyes as he hopped from foot to foot in his excitement. She took a deep breath. "What if you paid him in riding lessons?"

"Yeah!" Gil yelped, liking the compromise.

Nate grinned. "Sounds like a winner to me." He held out his hand to Gil. "Shake on it. I hire your services and will in turn teach you to be a first-rate horseman."

Gil turned solemn, then put his small hand in Nate's and shook like a little man. "Sounds like a winner to me," he said, repeating Nate's words. And Polly had to fight off an unreasonable wave of jealousy. Not for herself but for Marc. These were life lessons he should have been teaching his son.

She allowed herself to feel the grief for what he was missing, then she pushed it aside and smiled at her son.

He was happy. That was what counted. Nate Talbert was a good man and her son had begun to think the world of him.

Her first impression of Nate had been that he was a stern man with little patience. She'd been wrong. Nate would make a great dad. The thought popped unbidden into her mind.

Someone else's dad, she tagged onto the thought. Gil was Marc's son.

Chapter Eleven

"Did you know that Nate used to be in the rodeo?" Gil asked the next morning, looking up at her from where he knelt rubbing Bogie's belly. They were on the porch and the dog was eating up the attention as he lay sprawled on his back.

Polly fiddled with the strap of her purse and watched Nate pulling up the drive.

She still wasn't sure how it had happened, but somehow in the course of the evening Gil had invited Nate to go to church with them. Sunday school, then church after, to be more exact. They'd not been to Sunday school yet. Somehow that had turned into Nate picking them up.

"No, I didn't know that." But she'd assumed it. She also assumed that before long she would know every detail of Nate Talbert's life. She would know it because her son couldn't stop talking about him. And if he spent more time with Nate, she had realized last night

as she sat on Gil's bed and listened to his prayers—
which included thanking God for Nate—she was just
going to have to get used to it.

Her stomach had a wobbly feel to it as Nate's truck
stopped in front of the house. God had blessed her by
making them neighbors, giving Gil the opportunity to
have a male influence right next door—what more could
she ask? Not just an influence, but a great influence.

Still…

"Hey, Nate," Gil called, bounding off the porch.
Polly followed, feet dragging childishly as Nate got
out of the truck. He was dressed in starched gray jeans
and a pristine white dress shirt with steel-gray piping
in western detailing along the pocket and cuffs. He
looked handsome, but when Polly met his eyes she
realized something wasn't right. He looked as troubled
as she felt.

"You look nice," he said.

His gaze drifted over her and Polly's heart started
racing. It had been a long time since a man's compliment had caused her to feel something. She immediately thought about how his hand had felt on her arm
the evening before. To her dismay, she felt a heated
flush creep up her throat. "Thank you," she said, then
led the way to the truck.

Nate followed her and reached to open the door
before she could. "Thank you," she repeated, because
she was uncharacteristically tongue-tied. And all because she was overreacting to a simple, obligatory
pleasantry!

Nate seemed oblivious to her flushed face and incoherence as he opened the truck door for her. In fact, as they drove toward town with Gil filling the silence, she became more certain that her first impression when he'd come for them had been correct. Something was troubling Nate. He seemed distant as he listened to Gil, and though he answered every question thrown at him, Polly could tell he was working hard to hide his preoccupation.

The parking lot was full when they arrived.

"Sunday school is in the building at the side," Nate said, nodding toward the building.

"Thanks, Nate! I told you it'd be easy," Gil said, scrambling out of the backseat. "There's Max," he yelped before his feet hit the ground. Immediately forgetting his mother and Nate, he raced away.

Polly felt guilty that she'd been lax in attendance. It hadn't been fair to Gil. "He's always loved Sunday school," she said, stepping out of the truck, glancing over at Nate. His fingers were still wrapped firmly around the steering wheel. "Are you coming in?" she asked, suddenly realizing that he didn't look like he was.

"I've got a cow that needs checking over on some acreage I lease. I need to do that, then come back."

He really wasn't coming in. Stunned, she stepped back from the truck. It was irrational. He'd only driven them in because Gil had asked him to, but still, she felt abandoned.

"Then I guess I'll see you," she said.

He didn't look at her, just nodded, pressed the clutch and shifted into Reverse. "I'll be back."

Perplexed, she closed the door. His expression said

otherwise. Gil called her name and she glanced toward where he was talking with Norma Sue. Still puzzled by Nate, Polly thought maybe she should ask if there was anything she could help him with, but when she looked back he was already driving away.

"Thought for a moment Nate might actually come to Sunday school," Norma Sue said, coming up beside Polly, startling her out of her musings.

"He said he had a cow to check on," Polly said in his defense.

"Isn't that convenient? Ranchers always have a cow to check on. 'Course, I'm not one to judge the boy. Thank the good Lord I still have my Roy Don and haven't had to walk in the same shoes as you and Nate. Can't say walking into church alone would be an easy thing to do."

Polly felt the tug of emotion from the words that she understood so well. Was Nate having the same trouble as she was?

"I'm glad to see you show up, though." Norma Sue gave her a one-armed hug. "How's it going?"

They started walking toward the annex and instantly, like every Sunday since Marc's death, the same sense of dread sank over her.

It settled heavier around Polly with each step toward the building. "We're settling in nicely." At least that was true. If only it were true for everything. She hated this, and had begun to think it would never get easier.

"When do you expect to have the bed-and-breakfast open for business?"

With all that they'd talked about at the dinner, the

actual opening date hadn't come up. Polly focused. "I'm taking reservations for the summer fair the last week of May."

"Great! If it has the turnout that we had last year, you'll be able to rent out every room and then some."

Polly momentarily forgot her rising trepidation. "That's what I'm counting on."

"Wonderful! Seven weeks and counting, and things are looking better around here every day. Morning, Brady."

Mule Hollow had its fair share of good-looking cowboys and the sheriff was one of them. He'd been talking with Gil and his friend Max and the boys were obviously excited about whatever it was they'd been discussing. Polly shook his hand and smiled at the giant of a man. The first time she'd met him she'd thought of Matt Dillon and had the confident feeling that Mule Hollow was in very competent hands with him looking out for its safety and well-being.

"Mornin', ladies. Let me get this door for you."

"Mom, Sheriff Brady says him and Nate used to swim in that pond by our house when they were kids."

Polly cringed. "Well, don't get any ideas." The last thing she wanted was to have to worry about Gil jumping in the murky little pond.

"Aw, Mom!"

She slapped her hands to her hips and looked firmly at him, her nerves getting the better of her. "Gilbert Marcus McDonald, you will do as I say."

His expression fell and he looked at her sullenly. "Not the name. Mom—"

"No back talk, young man. You *will* mind me. Is that clear?" Especially when it came to dangerous things, she almost tagged on, but bit it back. She couldn't shelter him forever and Marc would hate that she was trying to hold him back...but Marc wasn't here and she was his mom. She knew her nerves were extra shot with her anxiety about walking into church as a single woman. And she shouldn't take it out on Gil.

That weighed heavily on her as Gil's shoulders heaved. "Yes, ma'am," he huffed. "But I'm *eight* years old."

"Not old enough," she said firmly, though her mind was spinning with conflicting feelings about the issue. Gil, good boy that he was, looked from her to Max, shrugged, then raced down the hall and disappeared into an open doorway. What was she to do? She couldn't very well just let him climb on roofs and swim in tanks... She sighed. It went against her nature to simply let him flirt with danger. Not that she wasn't trying to ease up.

"Sorry about that," Sheriff Brady said, and did some disappearing of his own. Obviously, he felt the same way that Marc had felt, that boys would be boys and what didn't kill them only made them stronger.

"Men, they don't even think about how us women worry." Norma Sue patted Polly's arm. "Don't fret, though, boys thrive in the country. Rip-roaring and learning as they go."

"I know. That's why I moved here—so I could relax—and look at me, I'm still holding on as tight as I can."

"You've got a lot on your plate. Don't beat yourself up about it. Now, if you had a man around to bounce things off of that would make a heap of difference."

Polly's throat clogged. "Obviously it wasn't in God's plan for Gil to have that."

"Oh, honey, your life isn't over. You've moved to the right town to fall in love again. I'm telling you, we have a great bunch of single men just needing the love of a good woman like you. Nate Talbert is at the head of the list." Norma Sue smiled encouragingly.

Polly forced herself to breathe. In that moment Dottie Cannon, Brady's wife, came out of the classroom Gil had entered. She taught the class and had invited him the day they'd moved in. She swept gracefully down the hallway and interrupted the conversation with perfect timing. Polly sent the Lord a thank-you.

"Polly, I'm so glad you brought Gil to Sunday school."

"Oh, my goodness, I just remembered I'm supposed to take Esther Mae's place in the nursery," Norma Sue exclaimed. "Dottie, will you show Pollyanna where the adult Sunday school is held?"

"Sure, I will."

They watched Norma Sue plow down the hallway, her flowered dress flapping in her wake.

"You know, they're gunning for you," Dottie said, her navy eyes twinkling.

Polly grimaced. "Surely not. I mean, I know they've hinted about me finding a good cowboy. But trying to fix me up—they wouldn't do that. Would they?"

Dottie chuckled. "Don't kid yourself. They would."

Polly gripped the strap of her purse and forced a smile, hoping it would translate to her heart. "So what are my chances?" she asked, trying hard to play along, so as not to seem too panicked by the idea.

Dottie looked at her kindly. "Now, that depends on how you look at it."

Chapter Twelve

Lacy caught sight of Polly just as she was being directed toward her class, and hurried over to give her a quick hug of welcome before dashing to her own class—the couples class, as in married couples. As it turned out, Lacy and Clint taught the young couples class. Pastor Allen taught the senior couples, leaving only one other adult class for Polly. The singles class.

She took a shuddering breath. She had to get over this. For a person who'd been used to attending a couples class for years with her husband, walking into a singles class that was populated—at least two-thirds of the way with eager-faced cowboys—still unsettled her as much today as it did the first time she'd tried do it. It didn't matter that it had been two years.

But the reality was that she was a single. And there was nothing she could do that would change the fact this second.

Sitting out on her upper balcony last night, she'd watched the night sky and prayed. She'd claimed the Lord's promise—fear not, for I am with you always. She knew it was true, she just had to keep focusing on that. She'd prayed that she could overcome this stumbling block. She'd awakened with the hope that today attending church would be different for her. That today something in her life was going to change… She sighed. But, what had began that morning as a step forward for Polly had disintegrated before even stepping out of Nate's truck. Standing at the edge of the doorway of the class, hidden from the occupants' view, she felt just as much like a misfit as she always did as she listened to the joking and kidding going on inside. Lighthearted. The way singles were supposed to feel.

A wave of wistful longing rolled over Polly and she closed her eyes against the onslaught. She would never know that feeling again. Would she?

"Don't be shy, young lady," Stanley Orr said, stopping to smile jovially at her. "Nobody in thar is gonna bite you," he boomed loud enough for everyone in the building to hear him. Polly knew everyone in the classroom had heard his words, there was no way for them not to.

With no easy way to avoid the inevitable, like disappearing into thin air, Polly nodded and did as she was told, stepping around the corner.

All eyes were on the doorway waiting on her to appear. Yep, they'd heard Stanley, all right.

A rakish-looking cowboy in the front row patted the seat beside him. "Speak for yourself, Stanley," he drawled, causing laughter to ripple through the room. "I'm sorta partial to shy ladies."

She wanted to crawl under a rug but there wasn't one.

"Don't mind them," Ashby Templeton said from the second row. She was the epitome of stylishness, from the jaw length cut of her hair to her expensive dress. Polly had been introduced to her early on but hadn't been around her since. "Please sit by me. Dan—" she lifted a perfect brow at the smiling cowboy "—is a nice-enough guy, but he doesn't need any more encouragement."

Polly chose the seat beside Ashby. Dan the cowboy looked over his shoulder and made a charming face as he held out his hand. "Dan Dawson, darlin', and really, I don't bite."

Polly slipped her hand in his. "Polly McDonald, Mr. Dawson."

He frowned, his eyes dancing with playful teasing. "Please, call me Dan, or wound me for life."

She took her hand back. His charming antics made her smile, even as they made her uncomfortable. "Dan," she said. "I couldn't possibly be responsible for wounding you for life." There, she'd managed a semblance, though a horrible one, of flirting.

He gave a crooked Dean Martin smile and clasped a hand over his heart once again, sending the room into chuckles. It was a classic overused move but it worked for this cowboy. Polly glanced at Ashby who shook her head and looked less than impressed.

"Lost cause," she whispered, leaning close to

Polly's ear. "Mr. Good Times Cowboy is the guy to steer clear of."

Polly saw the flash of playful challenge in Dan's gaze as it settled on Ashby. "Now, don't get jealous, Ash, you had your chance at this cowboy. And, sugar, you passed it up. Remember?"

Ashby crossed her arms stiffly. "Several times, I might add."

There were sparks bouncing off these two like flint and steel. Polly looked around to see if she were the only one seeing them. She wasn't. Every eye in the room was on Ashby and Dan. It seemed something was brewing there. She immediately wondered if Norma Sue and her buddies had gotten a whiff of this or had instigated it. She was beginning to view everything as suspect.

Sheriff Brady came to the rescue. He strode into the room and took the seat at the front of the class, drawing all eyes. Dan shifted his gaze from Ashby to Polly, winking before giving his attention to Brady.

The lawman was the Sunday-school teacher.

She didn't know why that struck her as cute, but it did. She wondered if when he caught someone speeding, he sentenced them to attend Sunday school. Or maybe he sentenced them to sit in the front row. *That* might explain what Dan Dawson was doing here.

Brady welcomed her to the class and then invited everyone to introduce themselves. There were six single women. Two of them schoolteachers, three of them worked at the candy store, which she assumed meant they lived at the women's shelter, No Place Like Home, since the candy store was an extension of the women's shelter. Then there were ten single cowboys, and as they each introduced themselves she wondered if there was anywhere else in all of Texas where more charming single men could possibly be in one room. Mule Hollow was indeed a treasure for single women looking for good men.

She wished them all the best. She just didn't fit as one of them.

Still, she'd come to church with an open mind and hope in her heart of hearts that here she could learn to fit in. But, despite the warm welcome, the charming smiles, the teasing flirtations and her single status, nothing had changed but her zip code. She didn't belong in the singles class. At least not in her heart.

The knowledge sank over her like a sheet fluttering over furniture that had been put into storage. Furniture whose season had come and gone… She tried to fight off the feeling, but it was of no use. She made it through the hour, amid friends, listened to a very well-prepared lesson on the body of Christ, and how each person played an important role in the church…but she couldn't rid herself of feeling out of place.

What part did she play?

Despite her appearance as that of a single woman, she wasn't. She'd been a working, functioning part of a successful loving team…just as the lesson taught that each member of the church worked to make up the body of Christ. She and Marc had been united as one. And though Marc wasn't by her side, visible to everyone else, he remained in her heart. To be blunt, he still completed her.

Frustrations escalated and she spent the end of the class praying for the Lord to help bring her emotions back under wraps.

She knew now, no matter how it looked to the world, she did not and never would belong in a room of carefree singles looking for that someone special to share their life with.

She'd been there, done that. Happily. And there was no going back.

And so it remained, that though she was in a room full of friendly faces, church and Sunday school especially—was the loneliest place of all.

Gil had gone home for the afternoon with Max, and Nate noticed immediately on the trip home from church that Pollyanna was preoccupied. He'd slunk back to church after the Sunday-school hour and waited by the front door of the sanctuary for her and Gil. She'd looked upset when she'd spotted him, and he wondered if he'd upset her by not sticking around for the early hour of church. He'd tried, he really had…but the minute he'd pulled into that parking lot, he'd known he couldn't do it. If she wanted to be upset with him, then so be it.

He'd stopped caring what everyone thought about him the day Kayla died. He sounded like a broken record. But, walking into the church was hard enough, much less walking into a stinking class for singles. A couples class was no easier. He'd known it, but Gil had wanted him to go with him so he'd tried.

It hadn't worked.

And now Pollyanna was mad at him. She sat watching the pastures pass by outside her window, ignoring him. He didn't blame her. He deserved to be shut out after running off like he had.

"I don't know about you," she said suddenly. "But I need a good long bike ride."

"Excuse me?"

"I said I need a good long bike ride. I need something to cure this, this discontent that keeps overcoming me."

Confused, he glanced at her. She wasn't mad at him?

She waved a hand, the motion full of frustration. "I need the endorphins the exercise will set off. I just need a bike ride." She tapped her foot impatiently, growing more agitated by the second. Maybe her attitude had nothing to do with him.

"It's a good day for a bike ride," he offered. He rode his horse when he was upset, so maybe Pollyanna's bike did the same for her. Maybe he needed a bike ride, too.

She looked at him flatly, and he realized suddenly he should have been asking the obvious, giving her an opportunity to open up. "Is there something wrong?"

"No," she snapped. "Why should there be something wrong? We just got out of church. We're supposed to feel *happy,*" she ground out, her foot tapping quicker. He'd never seen her this way.

He turned into her driveway and headed slowly up the lane. Bogie hopped from the front porch and came barreling toward them. Nate had to slow done to make certain he didn't run over the pup. When he had the truck securely parked, he lay an arm over the back of the seat and stared at Pollyanna. She'd made no move to exit the cab. Instead she stared out the windshield frowning.

"Look," he said. "I've only known you for a few weeks, but I'm pretty sure I'm reading the signals right. Something is bugging you. Do you want to talk about it?"

"No," she said flatly.

"Okay—" he started to say, but she cut him off, jumping out of the truck and slamming the door.

What was wrong with her? Nate couldn't leave her like this. He followed her up the flagstone walk. She'd stopped beside the planters of not yet blooming tulips. "Pollyanna, obviously something is bothering you. Talk to me. You've talked to me before."

Her back was to him, her shoulders slumped as she reached out and gently touched the tips of the spikes. "I *hate* being here."

That shocked him. "You hate Mule Hollow?"

Her head slashed around and she cut her eyes at him. "No. I hate being a widow." She swung away, her body rigid. "I *detest* everything being a widow does to me. I loathe walking into a singles class. I hate having to look to the future without Marc and I despise having cute cowboys flirt with me." She held up a hand to silence him when he started to speak. "And believe me, I know how silly that sounds. But it's the truth."

Well, I'll be. Nate pushed his Stetson back and rubbed his temple. "Actually, it doesn't sound silly at all."

That brought her around to face him. She lifted her chin, giving him her full attention.

He shifted from one boot to the other and tucked his hand into his back pocket. "I didn't have cows to look at this morning. I hate going to Sunday-school class, too. It's hard enough to walk into the main sanctuary. But to walk into a more intimate setting like the couples class—which they've invited me to continue to be a member of, still that didn't help—I just can't do it. Not without Kayla at my side. The only thing worse would be to go to a *singles* class. I can't bring myself to look at myself as single. And like you, it's also not that I can't do it, but that I don't want to." His voice was almost a whisper as he finished. Even saying he was single felt wrong. Polly was watching him so intently and he lifted a shoulder. "I wanted to be Kayla's husband until I was old, fat and had a bald spot. I was supposed be a father by now. I wasn't supposed to have female veterinarians chasing me or matchmakers scheming to find me a soul mate. I already have one. So you see, Pollyanna, I don't think anything you've said is silly." That was the longest, most honest conversation he'd had since Kayla died.

He and Pollyanna stared at each other for a long moment, both lost in the past as the feeling of discontent pulsed between them.

Literally deflating before his eyes, Pollyanna sank to the step, her hand resting on the edge of the planter, her eyes pained.

"I'm so ashamed," she whispered, then, lifting her chin, she looked up at him with such sorrow.

Nate sat down on the step beside her, and fought the desire to put his arm across her shoulders and comfort her.

She inhaled a shaky breath. "I believe God's word is the truth. I believe Marc is in Heaven. I know that. I was there when he gave his life to the Lord, and I know…I know because of our profession of faith that I am going to see him again. And—" she splayed her hands on her lap and studied them "—and for that I am eternally grateful and happy." Her eyes flashed. "And I am. And most days I move forward…but sometimes I miss him *soooo* much. And it overshadows my joy that he is in Heaven." She paused, her breath ragged.

Nate could only nod as his throat clogged with emotion. He understood completely.

"I know that he would no more return to this world or shed a tear to return," she continued, giving a half smile. "Just think of the beauty he's seeing, of the wonders that are unfolding before him… But I'm tired of being alone and yet I don't want anyone else. I feel guilty if even the thought pops into my head. And I feel guilty for missing him so much." She couldn't believe she was telling him this. But she couldn't seem to stop. "I can't even imagine dating anyone other than Marc, and I resent, yes, God forgive me, I resent being here and having to think about it." She plopped her hands to her thighs and forced a smile. "But hey, as wishy-washy as my feelings are these days, tomorrow I'll wake up thinking that I've turned a corner and I'm going to be able to get on with my life. That I'm actually going to take two steps and not lose one the same day." She clutched her hands together and didn't look at all convincing.

He twisted around so that he crouched in front of her. It was a natural thing to cover her clutched hands with his, feeling the need to comfort this woman who seemed to be looking into his very soul and reading his every emotion, his every thought.

"I feel so much of what you've said. I think what we feel is normal and I've long ago stopped feeling guilty for the way I feel. We loved them and we miss them. They were part of us and death hasn't changed that for us. Despite what the outside world sees. Time is irrelevant when it comes to grief. And love."

She squeezed his hand, the green of her eyes melting with agreement. "Thank you." Her voice cracked but she smiled a sad smile. "I have felt so guilty thinking about what the Lord thinks of me, too."

"Why?" he asked, realizing that he still held her hands, but it had been so long since he'd held a woman's hand, he found comfort in the touch.

She sighed. "Because of what God did for me. Waking me up before it was too late."

"How so?" he asked when she went silent. She met his gaze, and seemed to pierce his heart. Of its own accord his gaze drifted to her lips momentarily.

"You see, I used to be a workaholic. I worked eleven- and twelve-hour days at the restaurant that I owned."

"You owned a restaurant?" He could believe it.

She laughed. "Yes, a little hole-in-the-wall, but I did a fantastic business. That's what I was doing when

I met Marc. I hadn't been opened long and he walked in one night with his girlfriend. I didn't know she was the girlfriend of the week until later, but the moment he smiled at me, I fell in love. Instantly. I was such a young romantic. The next night he came in without his girlfriend and every night thereafter." She faltered. "I didn't mean to get carried away with memories— though that is one of the things God did for me, setting me up with Marc that way. But where I was going with this is that I had worked so hard to build my business that even after we were married and we had Gil, I continued to work long hours. I barely made it home in time to tuck Gil in at night, and half the time I was so worn out on my day off that I was missing everything and didn't know it. I had such a treasure and I was letting it slip by me." She took a shuddering breath. "And then one Sunday afternoon, I was sitting in a chair, so tired I could barely think, and I was watching Gil and Marc wrestle on the grass. I felt God tell me to wake up and concentrate on my family. Gil was four at the time, but I saw him grow up in a flash with me at work or too tired to enjoy our time together as a family. It shook me up and I felt this overwhelming urgency about it."

She was staring at him so earnestly that Nate almost leaned toward her. Wanted to pull her into his arms and comfort her. The thought caused his insides to go still. "So what did you do?" he asked.

"I wish I could say that I immediately changed my life. That I stayed home with my family, but you know how it is, I thought it wasn't really a word from God. I mean, how could I be sure…? Instead I ignored Him. But thankfully I had such turmoil inside me about it, God literally wouldn't let me forget that He'd given me a wake-up call. After three weeks, I finally mentioned it to Marc. He was so happy, he was always telling me that he missed me, that he didn't see enough of me. But he would never tell me to choose, he was just that way. I only saw what it meant to him when I told him that I wanted to refocus my schedule so that I could be home more. I will never forget his elation. That was all I needed. I got my priorities straight and put my family first. I sold out completely at the end of the year, really convinced that I wanted to be home for Gil and for Marc. It might not have been the right move for some, but for me it was. We had a great two years. If God hadn't given me the gift of that thump on the head, I wouldn't have had those last two years of treasured memories to cherish and sustain me." Her eyes glistened with tears.

Without thought Nate reached and wiped the tear off her cheek with his thumb. "I'm glad He did that for you."

She sniffled and nodded. "Me, too. I'm so thankful that I listened or I would have had so many regrets to live with. But God knew." Her voice thickened. "He was so good to me and that's why I feel so guilty. I mean, that verse, *The Lord has done great things for us*—not only did he send His son to die on the cross for me, He gave me Marc, if only for a short time. He gave me Gil. And then He woke me up in time to…" She closed her eyes, her hand tightening around his, and her voice trailed away.

"So you feel guilty because God gave you the gift of realizing you had a wonderful life and you feel guilty because you wanted it to last longer?"

"Exactly." She sighed. "It sounds so selfish."

She glanced down at their clasped hands at the same time he felt self-conscious that he'd been holding her hands for so long. He let go and stood, suddenly needing to put some space between them. Overwhelmed by the emotion that swept over him.

"I don't see that there's anything to be guilty about. God gave you a beautiful life and there's no harm in loving it so much that you wish you still had it. I wish I still had mine." He turned to look at her. "Unapologetically."

She reached for the flower again, fingering one slender stalk. "I can't help thinking there is something wrong about feeling this way."

"Why?" he asked.

"Because if I can't move forward, there's no glory in that for the Lord. And if there's no glory in it for Him, then I'm just spinning my wheels. I have to find a way to be satisfied with my life as it is. I have to find courage to move forward all the way. And I will. It's just…I keep getting waylaid all the time. One minute I'm thinking I'm okay, the next I'm like this." She raked her hand through her hair and frowned. "Quite frankly, I'm tired of feeling this way."

Chapter Thirteen

"I know what you mean," Nate said. He wasn't sure he agreed with Pollyanna on all points, but there were similarities. "I feel like my life peaked with Kayla and that everything is downhill from here. I can't shake the feeling. I've been praying for the Lord to send me something else to wake up for, because as it is, I feel like I've got one foot in the grave right there beside Kayla."

Polly placed her hand on his arm and squeezed. "I'm so sorry."

He raked a hand through his hair, completely thrown by the way he was able to open up to Polly-anna. But she understood. "The truth is I'm not even halfway existing and I'm tired, too…but I can't fathom feeling better without Kayla."

He told himself that he was telling Pollyanna what was in his heart because she'd been through it and knew what it was like to love and lose. Essentially they were both caught in the same kind of limbo. He'd not been able to tell his closest friends, not even his brother, the things he'd just told Pollyanna. The only other person he'd ever been able to be this open with was Kayla.

But the truth hit him that since Pollyanna and Gil had come into his life he'd been waking up each day feeling more like his old self. And he liked the feeling.

"Nate, would—" Pollyanna started, then stopped, looking uncertain. She took a deep breath. "Would you like to go on that bike ride with me?"

Despite her body language, the question still took him by surprise. During their conversation he'd forgotten all about bikes. "A bike ride, huh?"

"I have an extra bike. It belonged to Marc. It's a great bike." She smiled and Nate felt as if the sun had just come out from behind a cloud. "Really, come on, it would be good for both of us. I just want to ride and not think about any of this for a few hours. I'm ready to have some fun."

He hadn't ridden a bike since he was in school... early years. But the idea appealed to him. "Sure, why not?"

"Great!" She clapped her hands together and beamed. "Do you own a pair of shorts and sneakers?"

"Oh, cowboys can't own shorts and sneakers?" he drawled, quirking a brow in challenge as he crossed his arms. He already felt the heaviness lifting from him.

Polly matched his eyebrow with one of her own. "I don't know, can they?"

Nate laughed, and felt as if he'd just taken his first

breath in a very long time. Maybe there was something to these endorphins after all.

Twenty minutes later Polly had her answer. Yes, cowboys could wear shorts and sneakers, *but,* everyone else had better be wearing sunshades. Nate's shorts were stylish enough, relaxed brown cargos, far from the formfitting jeans he usually wore, and his running shoes were great…but the well-muscled knee and calf that connected the two—oh my, oh my, that portion of leg was blinding it was so white!

"You don't wear those often, do you?" she said in observation, so happy to be feeling better. And honestly looking forward to a ride with Nate. He gave her a boyish grin, tugged on a ball cap and winked. *Winked!*

"Well—ah, little lady, as a matter of fact," he drawled, giving a dead-on John Wayne impersonation, "when a man's got a herd to see to, thar ain't much time for such *frivolities* as sunning his legs."

Polly laughed, feeling the stress of the morning easing. And she was delighted to see him this way. "You do a great John Wayne."

He cocked his head to the side, jutted a hip out and put his weight on his back leg, reminiscent of the actor, which would have really been perfect if he'd had on his western attire. "That wasn't John Wayne."

Polly's mouth dropped open. "You're not serious? It sounded just like him."

He shook his head.

"Then who was it? Oh, oh, it was Foghorn Leghorn

the big rooster from the cartoons. I always said he sounded like John Wayne."

He rolled his eyes. "Nope."

"But it had to be, it was perfect."

"It was my dad."

"Your dad sounds like John Wayne?"

"Yeah," he said, looking at her seriously.

"If you say so," she said slowly, suddenly realizing just exactly how handsome Nate Talbert was, standing there totally out of character…looking completely relaxed. As she held his gaze his grin broadened.

"Honestly, it was me impersonating my dad— impersonating John Wayne."

"Ha!" she laughed, and stepped toward him, giving his arm a playful shove. "You think you're so clever."

"Hey, you went for it hook, line and sinker."

"Funny, funny, funny man. We'll see who has the last laugh after you pull those bikes out of the back of your truck and put those Mr. Clean legs to work."

She spun and sashayed off his porch toward his truck. This felt great! They'd loaded the bikes into his truck, then driven to his house so he could change clothes. It was as if without saying so out loud they'd both agreed to let the past rest for now. Polly had exposed more of herself than she was comfortable with and she felt sure that Nate felt the same way. Yet it had been a relief to tell someone what she'd bottled up inside for so long.

Nate jogged past her, flipped around and jogged backward, smiling at her as he went. "You don't think a cowboy can ride a bike, do ya, little lady?"

She wrinkled her nose at him. "I don't know, little man. We'll have to see, won't we?"

He let the tailgate down and easily lifted her bike down. "I could get used to this. I think."

She watched his back muscles strain against the polo shirt he wore as he reached for the other bike. He was a very fit man. Marc had always been in perfect shape. She pushed the thought aside, feeling guilty but needing not to go there for now. "Don't speak too soon. I bet you won't be able to walk tomorrow, you're going to be so sore."

He set the bike down and threw a leg over it as if it were his horse. "We'll have to see about that, little lady."

Polly hopped on her bike and took off down his driveway toward the bend. "Come on, cowboy, show me whatcha got."

"Hey! Hold up," he called as he kicked off, wobbled and almost wrecked because he was watching her rather than where he was going. She was looking over her shoulder, seeing his near crash. She cackled with glee as she stood up on the pedals to get more speed. She heard him laugh behind her and was glad he'd come along.

Nate didn't mind trailing behind Pollyanna one bit.

He caught her at the road, still a bit loose, but with his leg-length advantage he figured once he'd caught her he wouldn't lose her. Wrong.

"So tell me," he said, when he pulled up beside her again a hundred feet down the paved road. This time he realized that he'd caught her because she'd let him. "Do you compete or what?"

She laughed, looking so much more carefree. Nate found himself unable to take his eyes off of her.

"No. I just like to ride. Look, someone's coming! *Quick,* cover your legs so you don't blind them."

He dropped his chin. "Funny. Ha ha ha."

She blinked, her expression blank. "I wasn't joking."

"Funny," he repeated, causing her to smile.

The truck slowed so they stopped alongside it. It was the Wilcoxes. Esther Mae scooted to the driver's side and looked over her husband's shoulder at them. "Hi, you two. Goodness gracious, Nate, I don't know if I'm more surprised to see you on a bike, wearing shorts or that your legs are whiter than my gardenias."

"Hank, save me here, would ya?" Nate groaned.

Hank pushed his hat back from his weathered face and let his gaze drop to Nate's legs. "I don't know, Esther, I think the legs win hands down." He chuckled.

"I'm with you, Hank," Polly chimed in. "I was afraid you would be blinded by them as you came over the hill."

"I see your point," Hank agreed, and Esther Mae frowned.

"Honestly, though, Hank, I don't know why you're laughing. Your legs haven't seen the sunlight for a month of Sundays… No, I take that back. We'd have to replace *month* with *year* for you, but a year of Sundays just doesn't sound right."

"Well, Nate ain't got anything to worry about because I'm not planning to give him any competition. My bird legs will remain safely hidden beneath my jeans, thank you very much."

"Oh, Hank," Polly teased. "I was hoping to talk to the fair committee and see about adding a five-mile bike race to the spring festival."

Nate frowned. "I thought you said you didn't compete."

"I don't. But that doesn't mean we couldn't add a little extra something to the festivities. I mean, what would be more fun than seeing a bunch of cowboys like you, out of their element on bikes. Seeing you looking so cute on one is what just gave me the idea."

Esther Mae almost elbowed Hank in the jaw as she got closer to the window. "Polly, are you saying you think Nate's cute?"

Nate grinned, seeing Pollyanna's discomfiture. She turned as pink as the shorts she was wearing, and she really looked good in pink. He lifted an eyebrow and crossed his arms over his chest, realizing that he was more than a little interested in her answer…the idea slammed into him like a two-thousand-pound bull. Since when did he care what a woman thought of him?

Her eyes widened with surprise, or dismay, he wasn't certain which. He had a feeling her words may have shocked her as much as they'd shocked him. A shy smile lifted the corners of her lips as her eyes mellowed and shifted away momentarily.

"Yes," she said in a halting, small voice. "I guess that I'm saying exactly that."

Monday morning the matchmaking ladies of Mule Hollow were all aflutter sitting in every available chair at Lacy's salon, Heavenly Inspirations.

"I'm telling you," Esther Mae gushed, looking around the room. Not only were Norma Sue, Adela and Lacy in attendance, but also Sheri Gentry, Molly Jacobs and Ashby Templeton. Esther Mae's matchmaking brain faltered on Ashby. They still needed to marry off Ashby, but so far the right fella hadn't come along…although there had been some sparks between her and that not-so-ready-to-settle-down Dan Dawson…Esther and the girls had been watching them like hawks. There were sparks and then there were sparks, and with Dan it was just hard to tell, the boy could make sparks fly off of an ice sculpture he was so—well, to put it bluntly, so charmingly manly. Kind of reminded her of Elvis. She'd seen whole flocks of women trip over themselves when he flashed his pearly whites. But this wasn't about Dan Dawson or Ashby, this was about Pollyanna and Nate, and never before had it been such serious business. She'd called this emergency meeting first thing Monday morning directly after happening upon them riding bikes the day before.

"Well what?" Norma Sue snapped. "Don't just sit there and keep us in suspense."

Esther Mae grinned, too excited to get frustrated with her old friend. "They were just so cute together. And they both looked happy. *Happy*, can you imagine? Nate Talbert hasn't had a sparkle in his eyes in three years, bless his little ol' heart. And the other day, she called him incredible. You heard her, Norma Sue."

"But, Esther Mae," Norma Sue said, setting her coffee cup down on the counter. "I'm with you one hundred percent that the two kiddos need each other and it would be a wonderful thing. But fooling with widowers and widows? Frankly, I'm getting cold feet."

Adela waved her hand from where she sat at Sheri's manicure table. "I was a widow."

Norma Sue balked. "You're different. I'm just saying we could mess up here. What if we meddle and they get hurt more than they've already been hurt? It could happen. Even if they are both good people. And then there's the boy, too."

Sheri nodded. "She has a point there."

A drum roll started at the shampoo bowl, a sure sign Lacy was deep in thought as she tapped her red nails on the porcelain and said nothing. She was sitting with one leg draped over the arm of the shampoo chair and her arm resting on the bowl. Everyone watched her think and waited in silence. Finally she nodded her blond head and her fingers ceased tapping. "I get where you're coming from, Norma Sue. And you, too, Sheri. But I've got a great feeling about these two. And I've been praying hard. It's not like either of them just recently lost their spouse. If it had only been a few months, or even only a year, I might hesitate. But it's been three years for Nate and two for Polly." She smiled, her eyes bright. "Like I said, I've been praying about Nate for a while and so has Clint, and I really feel good about this. You know I don't think anything happens by chance. I don't believe it was happenstance that Pollyanna and Gil moved in next door to Nate. He needs them and God knows it. And they need him."

"I agree," Adela added, drawing everyone's gazes to her. With Lacy and Adela both in agreement, the entire room knew to take notice.

"And then there's the idea about the bike ride. That was genius," added Molly Jacobs, who, ever the news reporter, had her pencil poised on the notepad she'd been scribbling in. "I could really get my mind around a great article on this. Readers would eat it up."

Norma Sue snorted. "You be careful there, Molly. We don't want another herd of wacko women coming after Nate like you brought down on poor Bob."

Laughter exploded as Molly turned fuchsia. "Hey, if you'll remember, if it hadn't been for me writing that article, my Bob and I wouldn't have come to our senses and realized we loved each other."

"That's right!" Lacy said, springing up from her chair. "God works in plain crazy ways sometimes. And I just *love* that about Him."

"You would." Sheri laughed. "You and Him are a pair to be reckoned with."

Norma Sue grinned. "Now, that's the honest truth. This bike ride would fit right in. Of course, there's the problem with cowboys and bikes. I mean, not many of them have bikes. 'Course, we could put them on horses, but it's funnier to mix things up a bit for them."

"That's very true, Norma." Esther Mae was the first to speak. "They would sure be cute, all those pale legs. Why, the girls would come, I can just see all the teasing. You know, romance starts with teasing many times." She sighed. "We could start it off by giving each woman who shows up a pair of sunshades!"

Molly was scribbling and chuckling. "I can see this is going to be fun."

Lacy walked over and pointed to the page. "You write something good, Molly. Love will be in the air, I just know it. When we add the bike ride in with the cow-chip-throwing contest and the three-legged race I just know we're going to hear more wedding bells chiming this summer. I can feel it." She looked around the room. "Just think about it, y'all. This will be my one-year anniversary of being here. Norma Sue, Esther Mae and Adela, your dream of reviving Mule Hollow is coming true. Just look at all of us newly-weds sitting around this salon... Ashby, don't you worry, we haven't forgotten you." She winked. "Just because we're concentrating on Polly and Nate doesn't mean we don't have our eyes on the lookout for your Prince Charming."

"Thank you for not forgetting about me," Ashby said. "I'm more than ready for my Prince Charming, and I can't even get a date."

"We'll have to do something about that," Adela said.

As usual Adela had been quiet, happy to listen to everyone else chattering away as she took it all in. Now she smiled. "Girls, what if we fixed the bicycle shortage by having the females bring the bike and we make it some kind of team effort?"

"Couples!" Esther Mae exclaimed, jumping up and almost knocking over the portable perm-roller bin in her excitement. "It's a stupendous idea."

Everyone looked at one another, minds whirring as smiles spread around the room.

Norma Sue was the only one frowning. "But I still think that when it comes to Pollyanna and Nate that this is one time that we should double up on our praying and not so much hands-on tweaking."

Esther Mae sucked in her lips and clasped her hands tightly together. "I just don't get what the big deal is, Norma. Widows and widowers need love, too."

Norma Sue rolled her eyes. "Esther Mae, I didn't say they didn't need love. I'm just saying let's double up on our prayer, proceed with caution and let the good Lord do most of the work."

Lacy batted her big blue eyes mischievously. "Don't we always?"

Chapter Fourteen

Nate felt like he'd been dragged behind a horse overnight as he eased into Sam's Diner. Deep in their Monday-morning checker game, Applegate and Stanley had been watching out the front window when he maneuvered himself out of his truck. They were now staring at him like a couple of keen-eyed hawks.

"Mornin', boys." Figuring more than his pride was at stake, he squared his shoulders and tried to walk as normally as possible toward the counter. He'd been up half the night fighting off charley horses. But, despite the knots in his legs, his spirits were high. Even waking to find that his water pump had gone out hadn't dimmed his spirits.

Watching him with those hawk eyes, Applegate rubbed his boney chin. "As my pap woulda said, it looks like ya gotta hitch in yor git-along."

Stanley jumped his checker over Applegate's,

chuckling as he did. "Looks to me like bike ridin's hard on a body."

Nate grinned at the old-timers despite the rebellion of his calves and hamstrings, then grimaced as he eased onto the stool at the counter. Every muscle running from his lower back to his toes stretched and screamed at him. He knew firsthand that getting bucked off a bronc was easier than this. Sam plunked a coffee cup onto the counter in front of him and filled it to the brim.

"Looks like you could use this. What brings you ta town? We don't see you in here too often."

Nate pulled his hat off and set it on the stool beside him, having been too distracted by his aching legs to hang it at the door. And too sore to walk all the way back to the hat rack. "My water pump went out during the night, and since I don't do well without my morning cup of coffee, I decided to come see you boys' smiling faces."

Applegate's frown lifted slightly. "Well, it's about time," he shouted, tweaking his hearing aid.

Stanley looked from Nate to Applegate. "About time fer what, App?" he asked, cringing when Applegate's hearing aid squealed.

"Fer the young fella to see thar's life after—" He cut his sentence off and studied Nate.

"After?" Stanley's bushy brows met.

Nate's did, too.

"Stanley, don't be daft. The boy lost his wife earlier than I lost my Birdie and you lost your Elisa Jane and he ain't fared too well. But hol'n up out thar all alone ain't the way ta go."

Stanley spat a sunflower seed in the spittoon, light

dawning in his eyes at the same time Nate realized where Applegate was heading. Instantly leery, Nate took another swallow of coffee and rethought his decision to come to Sam's. It was exactly things like this that had held him back most of the time. Pollyanna had told him that she'd been hurt by people not talking to her about Marc after his death. But for him, it had been the complete opposite. Mule Hollow residents had wanted to talk about Kayla. It was he who hadn't wanted to. It was just too private, cut too deep—he thought about her every day, woke up thinking about her, went to bed thinking about her. But he didn't want to talk about her…at least he hadn't until Pollyanna had come along. He knew Applegate and Stanley meant well, they were both widowers, but Nate just didn't have the desire to discuss his life with the old cattlemen.

The door swung open, saving him from further discussion as a couple of cowboys came sauntering into the diner. To Nate's relief, Applegate understood that some topics were too delicate to discuss in a crowd. He stuffed a handful of sunflower seeds into his mouth rather than continue his line of conversation. Of course, with as loud as he talked they'd probably already heard every word he'd said. More than likely everyone all the way down to Pete's Feed and Seed had heard him. Nate's relief didn't last long. One look into App's wizened old eyes told Nate that he might have stopped talking, but that didn't mean he was done.

Nate took a swallow of the coffee, glad when Sam, who'd been keenly following the interaction, snagged up two mugs and headed around the end of the counter toward where the cowboys were sliding into a booth. His departure effectively gave Nate some breathing room.

"So, ya want some breakfast to go along with your new smile?" he asked when he came back.

Nate grinned over his cup, then took another drink. He should have known these three sharp-eyed gents would pick up on a change. But, though he'd made an improvement, he still wasn't ready to talk. About Kayla or Pollyanna.

"Nope," he said. "I've got to get over to Pete's and see if he happens to have a fitting I need stashed somewhere on those dusty shelves of his. But thanks for the coffee. Do you have one of those to-go cups handy?" He laid his money on the counter and picked up his hat while Sam filled the paper cup. As soon as Sam handed him the cup Nate headed toward the door. "You fellas have a nice day," he called, tipping his hat at the checker players.

"You do the same, Nate," Applegate yelled. "And remember, me and Stanley, we're here if ya need us. We might be old, but we ain't dead."

"Now, App, why'd ya go an' say an all-fired dumb thang like that?" Stanley scolded, glaring at his buddy.

Nate paused, nodding a greeting at the two cowboys who were now tuned into the conversation. Turning back, he faced Stanley and Applegate. "Look, fellas…" He fingered his hat. They really did understand. Both had lost their wives, and maybe he hadn't ever thought about the fact that he might have been able to glean some helpful wisdom from their journeys through their own heartaches. The Bible did advise for young men to learn from their elders.

He softened. "I really appreciate your offer." It was true. "Can I take a rain check today?"

Both men's faces lifted into smiles and they sat a bit taller. "Well, shor ya kin," Applegate said gruffly.

"'At's right," Stanley added, his gaze somber. "Any time you need ta talk you know where ta find us."

Nate's chest expanded as he realized he'd just done something that didn't necessarily have everything to do with focusing on his own loss. He'd never thought that letting App and Stanley share some of their journey with him might be a way of helping them, too. He put his hat on and quirked a corner of his mouth. "I'll do that."

He was almost out the door when Applegate called out. "I'd pick up some horse liniment over at Pete's if I were you. Else you ain't goin ta be able ta get out a bed tomorrow."

Nate chuckled. "I'll add it to my list, sir." Outside he took a deep breath. That hadn't been so bad after all.

He was just entering Pete's when he saw Norma Sue, Esther Mae and Adela hustling out of Heavenly Inspirations across the street. Despite the pain in his legs he stepped into Pete's faster than a bull out of a chute, so as to avoid them spotting him. From a safe vantage point, behind the red-checkered half curtain that covered Pete's window he watched the three ladies hustle down the sidewalk chattering excitedly all the way. He had to crane his neck to see them cross the street heading to Sam's. Whew! Talk about a close call. The only thing worse than getting put through the third degree at the diner would have been if the ladies had been there, too.

"Who you hiding from?" Pete asked, coming up behind him.

Nate looked at the large man and frowned. "Three guesses."

Pete let out a jovial laugh. "Say no more. I'd hide from them three myself if they were after me. But it's you they've got their sights on. Better get this order done, Norma Sue's got some feed lined up for pick-up any minute now."

Nate eyed the feed bags sitting on the sidewalk ready for loading and spun toward the feed-store owner. "Quick, then, I need to grab a few things to fix my water pump. Oh, and some horse liniment."

Pete grinned. "Heard about the bike ride. Don't you know horseback riding and bike riding don't exactly use the same muscles?"

Nate hung his head and cringed. "Yeah, but I just felt like going for a ride."

Pete boomed with laughter and headed toward the back shelf where he kept just enough hardware supplies to patch most anything that might go wrong with all things mechanical on a ranch. "That's a step in the right direction." His words echoed what Nate had already realized.

"You think so?"

Pete raised an eyebrow at him. "Sure. Means you're

stretchin' yourself. And though it hurts, it's a good feeling, ain't it?"

Nate thought about that. Thought about Pollyanna. "Yes, sir, it is. It's a real good feeling."

Chapter Fifteen

Polly was half inside the upstairs bathroom cabinet, painting, when she heard the familiar sound of Nate's truck pull up outside. Her heart skipped erratically at the sound and she jerked, hitting her head. "Ow," she yelped, scooting out from inside the cabinet. After placing her roller in the pan, she glanced into the mirror above the sink and cringed. She'd been working since she'd dropped Gil and Max off at school and had the paint splattered on her face and in her hair to prove it. Her heart continued thudding as she pushed her hair off her face.

"Polly's a pretty *girlll*," Pepper sang, watching her in the reflection of the mirror.

Polly stopped her primping and stared at herself in the mirror, feeling irrationally defensive. She wasn't primping. She wouldn't want anyone to see her this way. It was a normal reaction to look in the mirror and tidy up.

It was perfectly normal.

She'd found herself thinking about Nate over the last couple of days. It had amazed her that they'd had such a good time riding bikes together. But, more important, they'd seemed to have eased each other's burdens by voicing the fears and resentments that plagued them. And by voicing how much they still loved Marc and Kayla it had made them…comfortable with each other. It was important that Nate knew how much she'd loved her husband.

Nate's love for his wife touched Polly. Deeply.

It also relieved her somewhat to know that someone else could love their dead spouse as much as she loved Marc and still—she had a hard time even now thinking it—and still grow weary of carrying that weight around.

She'd felt deep down as if she was betraying Marc by feeling such a thing. It still amazed her that she'd opened up to Nate that way. And that he'd reciprocated.

It had been nice to loosen up for an afternoon. She'd really needed it. She wasn't sure why she'd been so wound up lately. She rationalized it was the emotions of the move and all that that entailed—leaving behind the place she and Marc and Gil had called home and starting over. The bike ride had helped. For a little while there she'd felt almost as if life was normal.

She'd actually teased Nate about finding him cute. The very idea still amazed her—both ideas, that she'd teased him and that she found him so attractive. But really, he was a handsome man, and there was nothing wrong with her noticing it. But that was as far as it went.

She swung away from the mirror, hurried down the stairs and opened the door before Nate had a chance to knock. "What are you doing here?" she blurted out. He was just lifting his hand to knock and he lifted a brow and slowly let his hand down.

"And a good day to you, too," he said.

Polly cringed. "Sorry, that didn't come out right." Boy, was that an understatement. "I've just been busy and hadn't expected anyone." She stepped out onto the porch.

"Polly's a pretty girl," Pepper called from inside. Polly snatched at the door and yanked it shut.

"Smart bird," Nate said, grinning.

Polly didn't know what to do with the backhanded compliment, so she ignored it and the tremor that raced through her chest. She refused to overreact. Still, looking at him, she felt off balance.

"I came to ask if Gil could go with me on Friday night to a campout?"

"A campout?" She repeated, sounding like Pepper.

"Yeah. Over at Cort and Lilly Wells's place. They hold these overnighters and weekend retreats for church youth groups, and they have a group coming from a small church in Caldwell. I've never helped before but they asked if I could. Pace Gentry usually helps, but he had other commitments come up. Anyway, I, well, I thought Gil would enjoy it. Max is going, too. And I'd take good care of him."

What was wrong with her? Gil had been talking about this. "It sounds like a fun time. Gil has been talking about it. I would love for him to go."

Nate's smile broadened. "Good."

Polly swallowed hard, looking at him. She'd gotten caught up in the moment on Sunday and had flirted with this man. Actually told him he was cute!

It struck her that those words were the understatement of the year. This man was far more than cute. Looking at him now she felt as if a feather had just traced down her spine. She almost shivered.

"Well, I guess I'll let you get back to work, then," he said after they'd been staring at each other for a few seconds. He turned away and headed toward his truck.

Polly realized belatedly that he was probably waiting for her to say something. She fought to quell the jittery way he made her feel. "Hey, cowboy, is that a limp I see?" she asked. It was the first thing that popped into her head.

"I owe you for that." He glanced back at her. "I've been in pain for two days because of you." His grin broke through the mock-serious expression.

She couldn't help laughing. "So sorry. But Nate—" she wrapped her hands around the porch railing "—thanks for listening to me melt down Sunday." That was what was wrong with her. She'd been embarrassed at how she'd acted after church. She'd been thinking about the way he'd held her hands and empathized with her. "I mean that from the bottom of my heart."

He swung toward her, his spurs clinking. "What are friends for? And while we're at it, thank you, too. I might be sore, but I think you're onto something with those endorphins. I woke up feeling better than I've felt in—" he paused, looking down at his boots then back up at her "—a long time."

The expression in his eyes made Polly's heart pound faster. "That's what friends are for."

They studied each other for a long moment and Polly felt her heart skitter, then free-falling. She looked away, but the free falling continued.

"Pollyanna," he said, drawing her to look at him again. As he held her gaze, it seemed as if he was going to say something more. But instead he nodded his head toward his truck. "I'll see you later. And thanks for letting Gil go with me Friday night."

Polly was glad to have something other than her crazy heart rate to focus on. "If he was coming around too much, you would tell me, right?"

"He can't come around too much. Pollyanna, I really enjoy his company. He's, well, he's good for me…and I think I'm good for him."

Polly took a deep breath and let that sink in. It was true, after all. "Like I've said over and over, thank you," she managed to say, her voice tight. She needed to stop worrying about Nate and Gil getting too close. He nodded, spun stiffly and ambled away. Polly watched him go, then turned to head inside, feeling as if she'd just stepped out of a spinning teacup at Six Flags Over Texas amusement park.

"So we hear Nate and Gil are going to the campout together," Ester Mac said.

The ladies had arrived early Wednesday morning, all decked out for gardening, topped off with wide-brimmed straw hats. Well, Esther Mae and Adela had wide brims, with paisley-print bands. Norma Sue had on a straw cowboy hat with a red bandanna tied around it. They'd been unloading Norma Sue's truck when Polly had gotten back from dropping Gil and Max off at school.

To say Polly had been surprised was an understatement. That truck had been packed to overflowing with plants from their own yards, and flats of new flowers. Obviously, the three ladies had gone somewhere and bought out a nursery.

They'd been plotting and planning for an hour on where to plant everything. Now they were busy working, scattered at various positions along the flower bed bordering the front porch. Esther Mae's comment was the first mention of Nate.

Polly paused in her digging. "Yes, he is."

"That's mighty nice of Nate to invite him," Norma Sue said. "We were encouraged to hear that Nate agreed to help Cort and Lilly in the first place. Only a few weeks ago, he would have turned Cort down flat."

"That's the truth," Esther Mae huffed. "That cutie-patootie suddenly seems to be getting back into the swing of things."

Everyone down the row beamed at Polly, making her squirm with unease.

"I think you and Gil have been very good for him," Adela added, patting the dirt gently around the periwinkle she'd just planted. "The very idea that you had him on a bike amazes me."

Polly smiled, hoping it didn't look as pained as she felt. "He's been good for Gil." It was the truth, and obviously everyone had noticed it. But there were these strange, selfish moments that she struggled to understand and deal with when she saw him with her son. Not to mention the way she'd been feeling lately when he was around. It was disturbing, but if she were really honest, it was nice, too.

Adela dug a new hole with her trowel. "You know, it's a pity Nate and Kayla didn't get the chance to have children of their own. Kayla told me once they planned to have a large family."

That didn't surprise Polly. It would have when she'd first met Nate. But not now. He was good and patient and so very kind with Gil.

"God's plan, though," Adela said firmly. "He always has a plan. Even if we don't understand."

Polly knew it was true. She just hoped they didn't get too carried away with thinking that plan included her and Nate becoming any more than friends.

She'd hate to disappoint them after all they'd done for her. But she'd warned them. And that was all she could do.

Chapter Sixteen

"He's here!" Gil whooped as he slid down the banister and landed at Polly's feet.

Gil had about driven her crazy over the past couple of days talking about the camping trip.

"Stop right there, young man," she commanded as he dodged her and scrambled toward the front door. His sleeping bag and backpack had long since been set on the porch waiting for this moment when Nate would come to pick him up. "I need a hug before you go off into the wild blue yonder."

He slid to a halt. "But, Mom, he's here."

Polly chuckled as she crossed to where he stood and engulfed him in a bear hug. Despite his hurry he hugged her back. Probably because he realized humoring her would be the quickest way to get out the door.

Releasing him, she followed him onto the porch and watched Nate climbing out of his truck. Her nerves kicked in as he strode up the walk looking handsome and fully capable of taking care of her son for the night. The man was totally male, strong and...capable. Her son would be safe.

"I'm ready, Nate," Gil said, scrambling off the porch loaded down with all his camping paraphernalia. Bogie followed him, prancing happily since they'd finally freed him of his clown collar.

"Okay, buddy, load up and I'll be right there." Nate smiled at her as he came to a halt at the bottom of the steps. "You doing okay?"

Polly nodded. "You'll take good care of him?"

His eyes held hers, steady and reassuring. "Like he was my own."

She flinched inwardly at that but hid it. At least she hoped so, but the shadow that crossed his face made her think maybe he'd seen it. "Good" was all she could say. She knew he would take care of Gil. Like his own. She took a deep breath. What more could she ask than that?

"Relax, Pollyanna," Nate urged gently, then surprised her when he took her hand. His touch sent a shock wave up her arm and she tried to pull away, but he held firm, looking at her intently. It was almost as if he could read her mind.

"Have a nice relaxing evening and I'll have him back by lunch tomorrow. I promise."

She nodded, then tugged her hand out of his, relieved when he let go. She fought the need to tell him again to keep him safe but knew she had to let go a little. "I'll be here," she said instead, and smiled. She knew he could see how tight it was, but he didn't say anything, just nodded and headed down the path. Gil was chattering away as they waved and drove off, leaving her and Bogie behind.

Polly watched until the truck disappeared from view, then she wrapped her arms across each other and stood there a little longer. She glanced down at the tulips that were almost ready to bloom and her heart skipped a beat as she looked back to the empty spot from which the truck had long ago disappeared.

Then finally, fighting off the uncalled-for unease pricking at her, she turned and went inside. She had work to do. Time was zipping by and there was still a lot to be done, painting especially, before she opened. Her son was in capable hands.

Very capable hands.

The following Saturday morning, Polly had her living room finished. The walls were a soft buttercup-yellow. Hands on hips, she admired the look of it. Bogie sat on the back of the sofa and appeared to be studying the effects right along with her.

"What do you think, buddy?" she asked, glancing at him. He wagged his curlicue tail and turned his deep chocolate eyes to look at her. Polly sighed. "I think that if you could talk you would tell me that you really like the effect of the glaze on the paint. Good, huh?"

Pepper was perched on the stair railing. "Pepper, what do you think?" she asked, sidestepping Bo and Sylvie as they crawled from beneath the sofa. Bo was pulling a Twizzler, teasing Sylvie with it. Boys would be boys.

"What do you think, Pepper?" Pepper mimicked.

Polly began humming "Old McDonald Had a Farm" and headed to the kitchen to pour herself a glass of iced tea. She'd awakened to the sunlight streaming into her window and the sound of Gil singing.

Gil singing.

Gil did not sing.

At least he hadn't for a very long time. His singing again was music to her heart. The camping trip the week before had been a full-fledged turning point for him. And much of that was due to Nate.

Nate.

Listening to her hum, Bogie padded into the kitchen behind her and flopped down, all four legs sprawled out, his belly flat against the varnished wood floor. He looked like he'd been squashed. Pepper flew into the room, landed on Bogie's back and watched her pour the tea over her glass of ice. It still amazed her that the dog hadn't tried to eat the bird the first time Pepper had used him as a perch. But he hadn't, instead he seemed to like it.

Taking her tea, she walked outside leaving Bogie and Pepper standing at the screen door watching her.

"Catch ya later, gator," Pepper called.

Polly's steps faltered. It was Marc's catchphrase, and though it wasn't something Pepper said often, when he did it always gave Polly's heartstrings a tug. It was as if the little bird knew the words were important.

Catch ya later, gator, Marc would whisper in her ear after kissing her goodbye and heading to work.

Polly took a sip of her tea, swallowing the lump in

her throat. She set the cup on the porch banister, her thoughts going to Marc. Happy thoughts. Still, her hand trembled as she picked up the watering pitcher, then walked out to the water spigot beside the shed. The niggling prick of worry that had stealthily hovered at the back of her mind for days tried to blossom. She ignored it as she'd been doing, humming instead as she waited for the pitcher to fill. Things were good.

Gil was singing. Gil was happy. She was good.

Bert came up to the fence, sticking his boney little head through the gate and watching her with alert eyes. He had settled into his area nicely as he happily devoured every bush and barb he could find. They'd replaced the rope latch with a chain that he couldn't eat. Still, Bogie kept his distance from the fence when he was outside.

"Bad Bert," Polly teased, When the pitcher was full she picked up her tea glass and carried it and the watering pitcher to the front of the house to water her precious tulips.

She was so thankful Bert hadn't eaten them before they'd banished him to his own yard. Soon they would be bursting with color and hope.

And a promise.

Marc's promise. Crazy guy, he'd always sent her tulips. They always arrived as soon as he and his friends left for an event, a race, a skydive…whatever it was they were doing that Saturday that he knew she was worried would put him at risk. The planter of not-yet-budding tulips was a symbol to her from him.

"Life is for living," he would say. "The coming blossoms promise that my love is always with you," the card would always read. Even if something should happen and he wasn't, it would imply.

In some ways she'd always hated those tulips. But she'd loved Marc with all her heart, and though she'd always thought his love of extreme sports was selfish on some levels, it was also part of his personality that she loved. Because of that she'd endured it and he'd loved her for it.

And now she didn't have him, through no fault of any stupid sport. But she had his tulips and his promise.

And they actually did give her hope. That was why she kept the bulbs each year and continued to add to them.

She'd come to look at them not only as a symbol of Marc's ongoing love, but as a symbol of God's promise to her, too. That He would always be there for her.

Today was a sparkling April day, and feeling the hope that the flowers always brought her, Polly lifted her face to the mild warmth of the sun. The faint sound of Gil's laughter surprised her and she opened her eyes, immediately spotting Nate and her son. After he'd come down for breakfast he'd raced over to Nate's early because he was going to help Nate fix fences. She hadn't realized they would be so close. They were down the hill working on Nate's front fence. As she watched, Nate placed his hand on Gil's shoulder and pointed something out to him with his other hand. The gesture sent Polly's heart spiraling.

They looked like father and son.

When Gil looked up at Nate she didn't have to be close enough to see his eyes to know that adoration filled them.

Polly couldn't breathe.

Her son had a major case of hero worship. And it was growing by the moment. All he talked about was Nate.

It was Nate this and Nate that.

Nate made him sing. Nate made him happy.

Gil laughed again and Polly felt like the sun grew brighter with the sound. Instinctively, she let her hand graze the tips of Marc's tulips, then her legs gave out and she sank to the steps, her heart suddenly breaking into tiny pieces. Her son was happy and it was because of Nate. But her heart ached for Marc. Someone else was getting the adoration that should have been his.

And that was the unreasonable thing that had been hammering at her for days.

Marc was gone. Marc couldn't teach his son to feed cows, or ride a horse. Marc couldn't watch his son grow….

Let it go, Pollyanna. Let it go.

It wasn't as if she weren't trying. It was odd, this protective thing she felt for guarding Marc's place in her son's heart.

It wasn't easy watching her son move further away from memories of his dad. She had to, though. She had to. She'd been praying about it. Praying hard.

Prayer could do miraculous things.

Well, almost.

Prayer wouldn't turn back the clock and make her

family whole again…and she had to come to terms with that.

For Gil's sake and her own.

"Nate."

Nate watched the boy as he tapped the dirt around the base of the post exactly the way Nate had shown him. He smiled, waiting to see what kind of off-the-wall question the boy was going to come out with this time.

After the fun they'd had at the campout he'd felt extra protective of Gil. Nate had promised Polly that he would watch over Gil as if he were his own. And he had. Pushing the guilt away, knowing it was unreasonable to feel like he was stealing Marc McDonald's blessings, he gave Gil his full attention. "What's on your mind, pardner?"

"Do you think my mom's pretty?"

Nate's hands stilled on the cedar post he'd been setting in the hole next to Gil. This was the last question he'd expected. "Your mom is very pretty," he answered honestly, picturing her sparkling green eyes and cinnamon hair. "Why?"

Gil glanced at him, then back to the ground he was stomping with his boots. "My mom's great. The best mom in the world."

Nate grinned at that. "You're a smart guy, even if you are a half pint. She loves you very much."

"I know. When my daddy died…" Gil stopped working and looked straight at Nate. His eyes, eyes that had been so full of excitement all day, were weighted with serious intensity. "My mom cried. She cried at night in her room when I was supposed to be asleep. But I sneaked to her door and heard her…and sometimes I still hear her."

Nate didn't feel comfortable talking about Pollyanna like this. But he also knew that Gil trusted him or he wouldn't be sharing this with him. "Have you talked with her about it?"

Gil shook his head. "I'm eight, but my mom thinks she'll make me sadder about my daddy dying if she cries around me."

Nate decided the fence could wait. He removed his gloves, pushed his hat back on his head and gave Gil his full attention. "Look, Gil. When you lose someone you love deeply, you don't ever stop missing them. Sometimes that means you need to cry. Even guys like us. How are you doing on missing your dad?"

Gil looked thoughtful. "I miss him…but…" His eyes misted. "My mom says he's in Heaven and he's watching me and that he would want me to be happy."

"And that's true. If you were my little boy I would want you to be happy."

Gil's forehead crinkled at that. "I think my dad wants my mom to be happy, too."

Nate was treading on swampy ground and he was ready to backtrack and run. But he wasn't about to leave the kid hanging on something he so obviously needed to talk about with someone other than his mom. And Nate did know more than he wanted to about what it felt like to be left behind.

"Gil, listen, son." He crouched down in front of Gil and placed his hands on his shoulders. "I'm speaking from experience here. You just have to give your mom time. But I'm sure your dad wants her to be happy, too. I would if she were my wife. That's what you want for someone you love."

Gil's eyes grew serious, his jaw locked and his lips slowly lifted into a smile. "I'm glad we moved next door to you."

Nate's heart, which only a few short weeks ago had been as dead and unresponsive as a rock, thudded in his chest and ached for this child. God have given him something to care about. "I'm glad you moved next door to me, too. Now, how about we finish this fence?"

Gil grinned. "Okay, pardner. I'm with you."

Chapter Seventeen

Polly was rinsing out her paint pan at the outside faucet when she heard a truck drive up. Bert was standing on his hind legs chewing on what was left of the honeysuckle bush. Ornery old Bert had turned out to be the best fence-line cleaner Polly had ever seen. Though she was going to miss the scent of the honeysuckle, she wasn't going to have to worry about unwanted creepy crawlers sneaking up on her or Gil. She shuddered thinking about it.

Turning off the water, she propped the plastic pan on end against the shed just as Gil came racing around the corner of the house.

"Hey, sport." She laughed, catching Gil in her arms as he almost bowled her over. After the day she'd had she was so happy to hug him. He was flushed when he stepped back from the enthusiastic bear hug he'd given her. "Wow, I'll take hugs like that any day, little mister."

"You won't believe it, Mom. We saw a newborn baby. A newborn! He was bawling and shaky and slobbering…it was so awesome."

She laughed at the way Gil's joy worked its way over every inch of his expression. Never in a million years would she grow tired of enjoying her child. Behind him, long legs and muddy boots came into focus. Lifting her gaze, she found Nate grinning, too. Gil sucked in a breath and kept on talking while their gazes locked over his head. She could see that Nate was enjoying Gil's excitement as much as she was.

"You shoulda seen it, Mom. I thought the mama cow was going to try to stomp me, but we moved *real* easy like." He demonstrated walking cautiously, his arms and legs moving in slow motion as he took a couple of steps. "Just like Nate showed me. Piece of cake, just like that she let us have a closer look-see at her little baby." He straightened and his expression switched to serious intensity as quick as flipping the television channel. "But Nate said we couldn't trust her completely 'cause of her horn-a-mones being all goofed up. So we kept one eye on the mama, just in case she spooked."

Polly stiffened, her gaze darting back to Nate.

"Don't look so alarmed, Pollyanna," Nate interjected. "We were safe. I promise."

She relaxed a little. Nate knew what he was doing, after all. And she knew he wouldn't put Gil in harm's way.

"It sounds like you had a really exciting time. Now, tell Nate good-night and go get cleaned up for supper.

We're having pot roast. It's been cooking all day just the way you like it."

Nate tucked his thumbs in his belt loops and watched Gil disappear into the house. "You've got a great kid there, Pollyanna. I know I keep telling you that, but it's the truth. You and Marc should be proud."

She smiled. Beautifully. "Thank you. I think I'll keep him."

She *was* beautiful. Inside and out. "Smart choice. So, how did the painting go today?"

"Quickly. I finished the upstairs bathroom, did a jig and sang a song of my own to Pepper."

He grinned at the picture she painted in his mind. He liked her this way. Happy. "Good for you. What's next?"

"The guest rooms." She crossed her arms and tilted her head to the side. "Would you like to join us for dinner? There's plenty."

"Not tonight, thanks." His stomach growled loudly. "I've got to drive out to Fort Worth on business and to see my parents while I'm there. I'll be gone until Thursday. Can I take a rain check?"

"Sure," Polly said, a tug of disappointment startling her as much as the relief it was tangled up with. She'd had an extremely emotional day. After the emotions that had attacked her watching Nate and Gil work on the fence, she'd had to do a lot of praying. She didn't have all the answers but she was dealing with it. She should be relieved that he was passing up the dinner invitation. That she wasn't was disconcerting. Her horn-a-mones must be messed up, too.

"Will you make sure Gil doesn't go around my place while I'm gone? He might get hurt or something and I wouldn't be around to help."

"I'll make sure. Have a nice trip."

He nodded, then left, and Polly hurried inside and called Gil to supper.

She could hear him upstairs talking to Pepper. She paused with her hand on the banister to listen to his excited voice, and though she couldn't make out what he was saying because his door was partially closed, she did catch the name *Nate* twice. It was hard to believe Pepper wasn't already singing Nate's praises, too. The man made quite an impression.

"Come to supper, Gil," she called again, and headed back to the kitchen. In a few seconds she heard him whoop with glee as he slid down the banister. Polly breathed a sigh of relief when she heard his booted feet thud to the floor. One more safe trip down the banister. She bit her tongue and kept her warning to herself. All the practice was probably making him better at it.

Gil raced into the room, Bogie trailing behind him. "All washed up, Mom." He thudded into the chair and placed his hands on the table with his plate between them. "Good boy." He laughed. "Look, Mom, Bogie wants his roast, too."

She smiled absently as Bogie sat at attention at Gil's feet. Gil had taught him that if he sat he got a treat. The pup had taken it to the next level by sitting before being told, expecting to still receive his treat.

"You are your father's son. You have his way with animals, Gil," she said, spooning meat and potatoes on his plate. "Before long you'll have Bogie talking to you like Pepper does."

"Whoa, that'd be too much."

Polly laughed and sat down. "Should I ask you to say the blessing or Bogie?"

"I'm the man of the house. I say the blessings."

She reached for his hand, loving him so much. "Yes, you are the man of the house."

After he'd finished saying grace, short but sweet and sincere, Polly thanked the Lord herself for her little boy.

"Do you know how proud your father would be of you?" she asked. She'd thought that would make him smile, but instead he frowned. "What's wrong, babe?"

He pushed his meat around with his fork. "I miss him, Mom."

"I do, too. But he would be glad that we're getting on with our lives."

"Yeah, I know. But, I was thinking about him today. Sometimes Nate puts his hand on my shoulder—" his voice faltered "—Dad used to do that, too."

Polly fought to keep her emotions in check. "Gil, about Nate."

"He's the best."

Polly set her fork down. It clattered against her plate. "Gil, it's nice that you—"

"I'm glad we moved here. He's like having a daddy next door. He said that when he gets back he'll give me another horse-riding lesson on Friday."

Polly's world tilted. *Oh, Marc.* Was this how it was to be? He would mention Marc in one breath and gush about someone else in the next. Eventually not mention him at all. He'd only been six when Marc died.

This day's emotional roller coaster was never going to end, Polly thought. Closing her eyes, she prayed that God would give her the strength to watch her son let go of his dad.

He had to move forward. He had to.

"Nate tells me you're going to be some cowboy," she said, willing her voice to sound bright. Once more, she reminded herself that Gil was going to need a good man in his life and if it wasn't going to be Marc...then she should be counting her blessings for Nate coming into his life.

When Nate got back into town, she'd just have to make certain that he understood what was at stake here.

She'd come to know Nate, to think highly of him. But this was Gil she was thinking of and she couldn't let anything fog her mind when it came to what was best for him.

Nate got back home late Thursday night, and as he drove up his drive he saw Pollyanna's lights on. He thought about going over and saying hello. But he didn't. She'd been on his mind the entire time he was gone and he wasn't quite sure about what was going on in his head. Or his heart. The one thing he was certain of was that he needed to go slow when it came to anything that had to do with Pollyanna and Gil. He saw her light flicker and wondered if she was moving around. He wanted to go over there and just see them.

To hear their voices and make sure they'd been okay while he was away. He wanted to look into Pollyanna's eyes and see if maybe she'd missed him, too. How had he, in such a few short weeks, become this attached to them? *Attached* was too light a term. He'd realized while he was away that he cared. He cared more than he'd believed possible.

Slowly. He had to take this slowly.

Everyone involved could get hurt if he didn't.

Gil came over the next afternoon straight after school and again first thing Saturday morning. But he didn't see Pollyanna. Gil told him she was painting.

On Sunday, Nate had actually wanted to attend church…even wanted to go to Sunday school, if it meant he'd finally get to see Pollyanna. But he'd had a cow in trouble giving birth and had to miss church while helping with the birth. He'd even had to call in Susan Nash to come out and help. By the time she'd arrived, he'd managed to save the calf himself. She'd looked after the mother and checked the baby out, and before she'd left, she'd asked him out again.

Susan wasn't all that bad. She was a nice lady, when given a chance. But, as he'd turned her down, he'd almost told her the same excuse he'd always given her—that he wasn't ready to date. But his words had stuck in his throat. They'd have been a lie. Up until a few weeks ago it would have been true…but not so now. He'd given it a lot of thought and he was ready to date. But only a cinnamon-haired beauty he couldn't stop thinking about. The question was, what would Pollyanna do if he asked her out?

* * *

Polly couldn't find her car keys. Obviously Bogie had been at it again. She had been searching for her keys for the past ten minutes and she was going to be late if she didn't find them soon. Where could the pup have hidden them?

The sound of a truck coming up the drive had her walking to the front door. Bogie, who'd been lounging on the back of the couch like a fat cat, jumped to attention and bounded off the couch and out the door the moment she opened it. The crazy dog had grown as attached to Nate as Gil and had learned the sound of his truck.

She watched Nate bend down to pet the wiggling pup. And grudgingly she admitted that her heart was doing odd things in her chest. That she was as excited to see him as Bogie. It had been almost a full week. She'd been busy since he'd gotten back from his trip to Fort Worth and obviously he had been busy himself. She'd found herself trying to make up an excuse to go over and see him, but she'd come to her senses and kept working. Ridiculous. And scary. And just plain worrisome.

Watching him walk up the path, she forgot about looking for her car keys and had the uncanny need to hurry out to him and give him a hug. Okay, she'd missed him. Friends missed friends. Right?

It seemed strange and impossible. She'd known him for a short month and yet it seemed like forever.

"Hi," he said, scooping off his hat and clutching it between his hands. She drank him in the way she would the first day of summer after a dark winter. He looked sensational. What in the world was wrong with her? She watched the black Elvis curl that fell across his forehead, then dropped her gaze to his smile. He had such a warm smile. Unlike when she'd first met him, he seemed to smile freely these days.

"Hello, yourself, stranger," she said. Her voice wobbled like the butterflies fluttering in her stomach.

He actually seemed to grow red beneath his tan. The man might have the whitest legs in Texas, but his face and arms were a deep golden tan from his hours in the saddle. She was positive that now there was a tinge of rose in that tan that had nothing to do with sunburn.

Being honest, she'd told herself that the reason she wanted to see him was to talk to him about her worries over Gil getting so attached to him, but looking at him, she wasn't certain if that was the entire truth. *Gil!*

"Oh, goodness! I'm sorry, do you want to come in? I've lost my car keys and its past time for me to leave and go pick the boys up from school, so I need to get back inside and search for the keys or else I'm going to be horribly late." She spun toward the house.

"I could take you, or go pick them up for you."

She placed her hand on the screen door. "Oh, no, I'd hate to impose."

He put his hat back on. "Pollyanna, get what you need and come on."

His obvious exasperation had her hesitating, but the boys did need to be picked up.

"I'm sorry," he said. "You and Gil are not an imposition to me. Okay?"

The look in his eyes shot deep. She felt like she needed to apologize to him. "Okay. I'm sorry. Let me grab my purse."

A few minutes later they were driving down the road in silence. Polly was lost in thought trying to figure out the best way to talk to him not only about Gil but about this entire confusing thing that was happening. She'd thought about it a lot while he was gone. And after all Nate had done for them, she wondered if he'd feel hurt that she would even think she needed speak to him about Gil. She wasn't sure what he'd say about her…maybe she was worrying unnecessarily that he was starting to have feelings for her.

"Pollyanna," he said after about five miles.

"Yes?" she snapped, feeling immediately foolish at her jumpy answer.

"I've been thinking. The thing is, this weekend is Cassie and Jake's wedding. And you know how we said it's hard going to events like that alone."

"I am getting better at it. But I don't know if I'll ever like it." Even the thought had her heart suddenly pounding away. At least that was how she explained the sudden erratic pounding.

"Yeah, me, too. I was thinking maybe I could drive us all there together."

She hadn't planned on going for that reason. Through no one's fault, she'd felt like a fifth wheel again on Sunday.

Nate offered an alternative. He seemed nervous.

"Don't look so scared," he said when she didn't immediately answer.

She shot him a glance. "Sorry. I know it would just be two friends helping each other out. Nothing more. I just suddenly got worried that the ladies might start getting the wrong idea."

Nate didn't take his eyes off the road. "They'll get over it."

His knuckles were white on the steering wheel. This wasn't easy for him, either. "Okay, I'll go." She nodded when he looked at her for confirmation. "So, tell me about your trip," she said, changing the subject. And she was genuinely interested in what he'd been doing since she'd seen him. It seemed like it had been ages and ages.

He smiled, probably from relief, and told her about his family. She enjoyed listening to him talk about his parents and his brother. "What?" he asked after telling her how his mother had fixed all of his favorite foods because she worried about his not eating right and that she'd sent him home with a ice chest full of casseroles. "What?" he asked again, when Polly continued to stare at him after her chuckles died away.

"I was just thinking that mothers never stop worrying. And I bet she's right, you don't eat well, do you?"

He dropped his jaw. "And how would you know that?"

"Just a good guess. You were at my house the other night and your stomach was growling. What did you go home and eat? And what did you have for lunch?"

He watched the road; his jaw flexed twice, then he slid his gaze back to her. "I forgot to eat lunch, I was busy. And I went home and had a peanut butter sandwich."

"Is that a habit?"

His expression hardened. "What's with the twenty questions?"

"I don't know. Maybe you should start cooking. I know if I didn't have Gil to think about I would probably not eat right, either. But having Gil makes me aware of needing things like food. He gives me an anchor that I need. I just worried—"

The school came into view. "Don't worry about me, I can handle myself. I've got one mother already. I don't need another."

"Hey, don't get mad. I was just making an observation."

"Yeah, well, don't."

The anger in his tone shocked her. "Aren't you the grumpy one today?"

His expression dark, he pulled into the parking lot. Polly spotted Max and Gil immediately. They were standing in a group of kids laughing and talking. Telling tall tales, probably.

"Nate."

He didn't look at her. Instead he watched Gil, too.

"What?" he asked after a brief hesitation, anger still lacing his tone.

Something was really bothering him, she realized. He was wound tight. Exactly what was going on in his head? She stared at him and took a stab at the heart of what motivated his moodiness. "She would want you to move on. To eat right, take care of yourself. Find another wife."

Anger swift and dark shadowed his eyes. "You don't know what she'd want."

Irrationally, Polly felt driven suddenly. "Yes, I do. If it had been me who died in the car crash instead of Marc, I would want him to find happiness again. I would want him to remarry someone to share his life with. Someone to take care of him."

"What is your obsession with men needing to be taken care of? What about you?"

Gil and Max were jogging toward them. "Me? Well, it's different. But you, men, God made a man to have a helpmeet."

Anger flashed in his eyes. "I had one. He took her away. Now, can we not talk about this?"

Polly opened her door and hopped down from the truck and let the boys scramble in. There was no need for Nate to worry about their conversation continuing. Max and Gil were so excited that Nate had come to pick them up that they talked nonstop all the way home. Thankfully they were completely oblivious to the tension radiating between Polly and Nate.

It gave Polly time to ask herself what in the world had she been thinking?

Who was she to be trying to run Nate's life? And what was that all about telling him he needed to get married! If he'd have said that to her she'd have been mad, too.

Polly watched him with her son and his friend, answering their questions, laughing at their jokes. Nate lit up when Gil was around. It was instantaneous and the feelings were mutual.

They'd seemed linked from the beginning.

So there. Her reasoning for interfering in Nate's

life was because he was her friend and Gil's, and friends were supposed to be concerned for each other. Right?

And she had a right to do so, if he was going to be an important person in Gil's life.

Was he going to be an important person in Gil's life?

Was she going to butt out and let this play out however it was supposed to play out?

Yes. Despite her worries and her fears she was going to have to back down. Nate was *already* an important person in Gil's life.

Chapter Eighteen

It had been a long day. After dropping Pollyanna and the boys off at her house, he'd spent the rest of the afternoon searching for a lost calf. Then he'd dug postholes until dark. Gil had wanted to come along but he'd needed to be alone. He'd needed the exertion, needed the mindless repetition and the hard work that stole everything out of him and left no room for thoughts.

But the thoughts had just waited on him. They were hidden in the recesses of his mind and ambushed him the minute he'd laid his shovels down. Knowing it was useless to continue to put off confronting his demons, he trudged into his empty kitchen and made a strong pot of coffee. After he'd washed off some of the grime, hot cup in hand, he hunkered down in his swing.

His and Kayla's swing.

He'd given it to her for Valentine's Day, and they'd

spent many evenings side by side, drinking their coffee and watching the sunset.

Three years now he'd spent drinking coffee alone in their swing, watching sunset after endless sunset.

He was growing to hate sunsets.

Tonight the sun had already gone down and he stared sullenly out over the back pasture bathed in moonlight, feeling the heavy pull of loneliness, heavier with each passing day. He missed Kayla's touch, he missed her laugh, but most of all he missed their conversations. Something so easily taken for granted…the simple act of sharing his daily routine with the one he loved.

He ached for that again.

Pollyanna stepped into his thoughts the way she'd been doing over and over again. Rolling the empty cup between his hands he stood and paced the length of the porch. He'd gotten irrationally angry today.

He'd used the wedding as an excuse to test the waters. He'd thought he was asking her on a date. The last thing he'd wanted from Pollyanna was for her to mother him. He scrubbed his eyes with his fist before raking his hand down his face.

She'd looked at him with such a startled expression that he'd buckled and told her it was just as friends.

Coward.

Who was he kidding? He wouldn't even know what to do on a date. It had been ten years since he'd asked Kayla out the first time. He was pretty rusty. And what did it matter? Pollyanna wasn't interested in a date.

He leaned his head back and let out a long, frustrated sigh. He was tired.

Tired of sitting here night after night on the porch with nothing but memories.

His heart started hammering with guilt. He closed his eyes and could almost feel Kayla's hand against his heart. Almost. Tonight she seemed far away, out on the edge of his memory looking in. It had been happening subtly over the past few weeks.

Nate had never been a coward. But he felt like one now. And he wasn't sure what he was scared of. Was it what Pollyanna had talked about? That Kayla's memory would pull further and further away? That she would become like a shadow in the mist. And that he couldn't do anything about it.

Or was it that he knew deep down it was time for him to make the move. That it was time for him to stop using Kayla and his guilt as a crutch. She would want him to remarry.

Yup. True.

As he stared up at the dark sky, his heart felt twisted and as volatile as the fury of a tornado shredding open ground.

Kayla had been gone for three years. He felt as if he'd curled up and hibernated ever since. Pollyanna and Gil had changed that.

He wanted them. Guilt free. He wanted them.

As plain as that. But they weren't his to have unless Pollyanna could let go of Marc.

Unless she fell in love with him the way he'd fallen in love with her.

He let the admission settle in around him. He loved Pollyanna McDonald. And it didn't take away any of his love for Kayla.

That was the astounding thing.

But could Pollyanna ever feel this way? Nate could only pray that God would open her heart.

On Saturday afternoon, to the rhythmic rendition of "Jesus Loves Pepper," Pollyanna waited nervously for Nate's truck as it eased up her lane. He was coming to pick them up for the wedding. After having made him so angry, she hadn't been sure he still wanted her to go, but he'd called on Friday to apologize for his bad behavior and assured her that he wanted to escort her to the wedding if she'd still allow him to. She'd forgiven him before he'd called. But it pleased her that he did, explaining as she'd already assumed, that he'd had a lot on his mind and it hadn't been her that he was frustrated with, but himself.

But what had she been thinking, anyway? The man did need to eat better. He needed someone to take care of him, but what business was that of hers?

She was certain someone would come along who would be glad to worry about Nate. Polly thought about Susan Nash. The female veterinarian would be more than happy to step in and worry about Nate.

Bogie came scrambling around the corner of the kitchen, signaling that Nate was coming up the drive. The ruckus he started sent Pepper into hysterics and Polly's heart joined in with all the sudden commotion. Walking to the door, she placed a hand on her queasy stomach, only then realizing how nervous she was about going to the wedding. Or was it about going with Nate? Because despite every reason she debated for going, this almost seemed like a first date to her.

Of course she knew it wasn't. Despite the fact that she thought it would be good for Nate to find a wife— again, it was no business of hers. Still, Nate was no more thinking about dating than she was…so, then, what was wrong with her?

As she watched him stride up the walk, her mind went blank.

The man was gorgeous was the only thing she was thinking as she opened the door to him. She took a deep breath, and fought to sound casual. "My, my, Mr. Talbert. Don't you clean up nicely." Did that sound like flirting? *Had she just flirted with Nate?* Polly felt crimson heat rise up past her neckline.

What was wrong with her? He was going to think she was a goof. She rubbed a knot that had formed below her earlobe. The tension in the air left her teasing statement hanging like a bad joke.

Of course, it didn't help that she was gawking at him as if she'd just been rescued from a deserted island after years of solitude! She'd seen him dressed for church before. But, she thought in her defense, today he wore black dress jeans and a Stetson, and a white shirt that shimmered just a smidgeon beneath the dove-gray dress coat. But it was the penetrating look in his eyes that would make any woman melt. She hadn't seen that look before, and quite frankly it caused her insides to flutter and her mouth to go dry.

Then he pulled his hat off, exposing that wavy black hair, and his lips curved into a smile that would make any woman melt. "Ms. McDonald, I could say the same for you, except it wouldn't do you justice."

She touched her temple, captured by the look in his eyes. "Y-you can still say it." She swallowed hard and tucked a curl behind her ear. Her fingers were trembling. Her stomach was, too.

His eyes swept down her. "You're breathtaking."

Okay, her knees began to tremble, too.

And her insides.

Something had changed between them and it wasn't her imagination.

The knowledge left her balancing on the edge of a precipice, feeling the rock shift beneath her feet.

"Hey, Mom," Gil called, sliding down the banister. He plopped to the ground as light on his feet as a cat. "I don't see why I've gotta wear this stiff shirt. It scratches."

Polly jumped as if she'd been caught doing something wrong and swung toward Gil. She forced her voice to work, praying she sounded normal. She did not look at Nate. "Gil thinks that if it's not Sunday morning he shouldn't have to wear a dress shirt and he's not too keen on it even then."

She couldn't meet Nate's eyes, but she glanced his general direction and caught him tugging at his collar.

So he was nervous, too.

"I agree," he said, sounding like a bullfrog. Polly

couldn't help looking at him now. He swallowed hard, meeting her gaze, then turned his attention to Gil. "But this is a special occasion, pardner." Gil frowned at him. "Cassie and Jake are getting married and we're dressing up in honor of them. That's what you do on special days. And when two people are lucky enough to find love, it's a time to celebrate." He looked at Polly.

"W-we, better go," Polly stuttered, and herded Gil out the door. Nate's hand on her arm stopped her on the threshold.

"Pollyanna."

Her heart was pounding as she looked up at him. He was watching her. "I agree with your reasoning," she said softly, and found her gaze drawn to his smiling lips. She did. He knew the power of love and commitment. And the beauty of the ceremony that said it was sacred.

"I know. Shall we?"

He led the way to his truck. After Gil had scrambled into the backseat, Nate held his hand out for Pollyanna's. Slipping her hand into Nate's, she forgot to move. She just stood beside him, cocooned by the open door, feeling the simple warmth of his hand clasped securely around hers. He didn't make a move, either. One hand held hers, the other was at the small of her back ready to support her as she climbed up into the high seat. Head feeling light, she swallowed slowly and lifted troubled eyes to his. She wondered if he could hear her heart. Wondered if he could look at her and know that she had suddenly lost her footing and was plunging headfirst down a rock face without a harness.

Chapter Nineteen

The little white church's parking lot was packed. As usual, Gil immediately ran off to find Max, leaving Polly and Nate alone to walk up to the church. Because of the crowd, they'd had to park down the road on the grass.

"The entire county must be here," Polly said, settling her purse strap on her shoulder. The purse strap was just fine, but adjusting it gave her an excuse to slip her hand out of Nate's the moment he'd helped her from the truck. He slipped his hand beneath her elbow and guided her forward along the road. His touch had her brain muddled.

"Everyone loves Jake and Cassie. They're really excited about taking this step into a life together. I'm glad we came to wish them well." He paused at the steps of the church and looked down at Polly. "Thank you for coming with me today."

"You're welcome. I envy them their fresh start. I remember feeling so happy and full of dreams," Polly said, meeting Nate's eyes. Shaken by the intensity she saw there, she started up the steps. He stopped her, tugging her around to look at him again. When he slipped his arm around her back and slowly pulled her close, her heart was beating so erratically she felt dizzy.

"Pollyanna—" he started as his gaze bore into her, "you make me want to dream again. To take those steps—"

"Ah-hem." Applegate Thornton cleared his throat, poking his head out the door. "You two coming in or ya gonna stand out thar all day?"

Polly whipped away from Nate, knowing Applegate was enjoying what he'd just witnessed. The twinkle in his eyes was too bright, and the twitch at the corner of his frowning lips too apparent.

What had just happened between them? Polly's thoughts were reeling. Nate had looked almost as if he wanted to…as if he wanted to kiss her. And she'd responded to what she'd seen in his eyes. His words.

Shaken but struggling for composure, she let his words sink in. She made him want to dream.

That's what he'd said. What did that mean, exactly?

Spotting the bridal party waiting at the door of the Sunday-school building, she waved and couldn't help feeling ecstatic for the glowing young woman in her white wedding dress.

"Hello, you two," Max's mother called as she hurried up to them. "We are so glad you both could make it. Polly, Gil is sitting with Max, I just checked on them, and since I'm bridesmaid and Dottie is the maid of honor and can't sit with them, I would appreciate if y'all could sit with them. Just in case they decided to start a wave or something when the preacher announces Jake and Cassie are husband and wife."

Polly nodded, glad to have a distraction, but more than aware that Nate had stepped close. "Sure," she managed to say.

"Great, see you after," Rose said, then hurried back to the wedding party.

"Shall we?" Nate said, leaning so close his breath tickled her ear and raced down her neck.

Polly swung around and took the arm he offered without meeting his eyes. She was feeling so off-kilter that they were inside the building before she registered that they were moving.

The church was packed and the pew they found the boys sitting in was so full they felt like sardines when they squeezed in beside them.

When Nate placed his arm on the back of the seat behind her shoulders, Polly told herself it was simply to relieve the tight fit of what seemed like twenty people on a pew built for ten. But she was more than aware of the man beside her. And his words would not cease rolling over and over inside her head. It was worse than Pepper repeating himself.

It was a lovely ceremony, despite Polly being distracted by Nate's proximity. The moment Bob Jacobs started singing a love song for the couple, the entire sanctuary went still. His amazing voice set the stage for a wedding ceremony as sweet and God-centered as Polly had ever seen. And it brought with it cherished memories of her own wedding. And the wish for something more.

Max and Gil didn't start a wave when Pastor Allen pronounced Jake and Cassie man and wife. But Polly found herself tearing up. "What's wrong, Mom?" Gil asked, looking up at her.

"Nothing, honey."

He scowled and looked at Max. "Girls are weird."

"Yeah, but they smell nice."

Polly dabbed at her eyes as the boys scrambled over her and Nate and hurried out the side door, forgoing the slow procession filing out after the bride and groom.

"It's easy to tell Max is a couple of years older than Gil," Nate said, leaning close to her ear. Again, his warm breath whispered along her skin and sent tingles through her. She shivered from the way that she'd awakened to this awareness of Nate. Her head was feeling fuzzy, and because of the crowd, the sanctuary was hot. Still, she shivered again.

"Are you cold? You look pale," Nate asked, seeming totally unaware of the affect he was having on her.

"I'm fine. I just feel like I need some air."

Looking concerned, he took her arm and led her out the side door. Polly took a deep breath and hoped it would help ease the odd feelings mixing it up inside her. She knew it was simply from the emotions of watching the wedding and remembering hers. That was what it was.

"Hey, you two," Lacy called, hurrying up. "You're coming over to the community center, aren't you?"

Polly nodded and Nate, too. Lacy grinned.

"Good, great, in fact. See y'all there. By the way," she called over her shoulder as she sailed by, "you two look really snazzy together."

Like a whirlwind, Lacy raced away to join Norma Sue and Esther Mae, who had slipped out early to beat the crowd and make sure things were ready for the reception. Polly figured Adela would have left with them, but she was playing the piano.

Polly was thinking about all these points, and trying not to focus on what Lacy had just said. She already knew she and Nate looked snazzy. Nate would make anyone look fantastic. The man was a walking cologne ad. With or without his Stetson. Still, they weren't a couple.

You could be.

"Mom, can I ride with Max?" Gil asked, skidding to a stop. He was moving so fast, he bumped into her. If Nate hadn't reacted quickly and caught her they'd have fallen to the ground in a heap. As it were, he wrapped his arms tightly around her and kept them on solid ground.

"Whoa there, pardner," he drawled, holding Polly steady while she held Gil steady. His arms were strong and she could feel his heart pounding against her shoulder as she looked up at him then back to her son.

Gil's eyes twinkled impishly. "Sorry," he said. "But can I, please?" If Polly hadn't known better she would have thought he'd knocked into her on purpose. But her brain wasn't sparking on all cylinders, as she was still shaken by the fact that Nate was still holding her in his arms.

Polly barely nodded but that was enough for Gil. He raced off, tossing a thank-you over his shoulder. She stepped away from Nate immediately.

"Is something wrong?"

Polly hugged herself, her hands clutching her arms in a death grip. "No. Fine." Like that sounded convincing.

"Look, I know you want to go to the reception, but can we walk for a bit before we head that way?"

Walking meant more time with him. Alone time. Polly met his gaze and her nails bit into her biceps. "Sure."

No, no, no! her better judgment squeaked.

Nate smiled and tucked his fingertips into the front of his jeans, causing his suede jacket to flair at his narrow hips. He looked relaxed and comfortable.

Polly was neither.

It didn't help that she was noticing far too many details about Nate. Like the way his hair curled slightly at his nape. And that when she stood beside him, her shoulders came exactly to the right level for him to comfortably drape his arm across them…a thought that reminded her all the more of the comfort she'd drawn from being held in Marc's arms. Only, she was suddenly having a hard time thinking of Marc. And for that she felt guilty.

Basically she was a mess. And he wanted to walk.

Which meant talking.

She wasn't so sure she could talk at the moment. Her mind was too full. She kept thinking about what Nate had said earlier. He said she made him want to dream. What had he meant by that?

"It was a nice ceremony."

His soft baritone eased a bit of tension from her and she nodded, falling into step beside him as he started strolling toward the side of the church. Behind them, gravel crunched as cars drove out of the parking lot and headed toward town.

"I miss the ease that I used to feel when I was here."

Polly glanced at him. "Did you and Kayla belong to this church long?"

He nodded. "I met Kayla at A & M. She'd inherited our house from her grandparents. But they'd used it as a weekend home for years, and it was pretty run-down when we decided to make our home here. We loved it, though…young dreams. That's what we had when we started attending church here and fixing up our place."

Polly understood about those dreams. She'd come to Mule Hollow to fulfill her and Marc's "young" dreams. What kind of dreams had he meant before the wedding? Was he saying he wanted to share dreams *with* her?

"Can we sit for a minute?" Nate asked when they came to a park bench sitting to the side of the small playground.

"Okay." She glanced at the iron bench. It seemed far too small, but she would have been silly-looking if she'd hugged the arm of it. Managing a smile, she settled as casually as possible beside Nate. Not so easy when his arm was draped on the back of the bench and his thigh brushed hers ever so slightly. Once again she was more than a little aware of him as a man. Not just any man, but a man she could—

"Can we try something?" he asked, cutting into the thought that she couldn't quite get into focus.

She looked at him, his dark eyes drawing her. He shifted so that his arm no longer draped behind her on the bench. Instead, his hand rested exactly between her shoulder blades. She could feel the tension in his knuckles through the thin material of her dress.

"I know the wedding was a sentimental journey for both of us. But can we spend the rest of the afternoon trying not to think about our past?"

Marc and Kayla. Polly stiffened.

"Please don't tense up again, Pollyanna. You don't have anything to be afraid of with me."

Polly wasn't so sure. His thumb gently caressed the spot where it touched her back, and she felt the gentleness all the way to her toes. She met his gaze, seeing the intense look she'd glimpsed when they'd first approached the church earlier. The pull was strong, magnetic, and she found herself leaning ever so slightly toward him.

"You make me want to get on with my life. I'm just asking for us to step out there and try."

"Try." Polly bit her lip. Could she?

He nodded again. "They would want us to at least try to move forward."

Her entire world revolved around those two words. *Move forward.* She sucked in a deep breath. Marc's words echoed in her mind. "Life is for living." He'd said it over and over, like a mantra. She blinked back the burning sensation that welled behind her eyes. She'd never thought she would even want to try after having loved Marc so much…but she'd never thought she would meet someone like Nate.

These unnerving feelings had snuck up on her. And they scared her. And what was new about that? Everything scared her.

"The last thing I want to do is hurt you," she said. "But more than that, I can't hurt Gil any more than he's been hurt. I'm already worried about the attachment he has for you. If…" She looked away. Nate took her hand between his two strong hands and squeezed gently. Drawing her to look at him.

"I would never hurt Gil. Or you."

Polly searched his eyes. "That's a promise none of us can make. We both know that."

"True. But are the risks worth it? I think so. I think you and Gil are worth it."

Polly hadn't expected this when she'd moved to Mule Hollow. She'd expected to settle in and grow content with the life she'd been given. She hadn't expected to fall…to find someone she could— She couldn't finish the thought. Couldn't bring herself to let the idea come fully into her consciousness. It might be back there, hovering, but for some reason, she couldn't think it. Instead, she shoved it away and stood.

"We can try," she said, and held out her hand.

Nate stood, took her hand and tugged gently, pulling her into his embrace. He cupped her head against his shoulder and whispered, "thank you," against her hair.

Trembling, she closed her eyes and for a moment

relished the feel of him. The strength of his arms, the steady, sure beat of his heart against her cheek, the gentle caress of his hand upon her shoulder snuggling her closer. For the first time in two years Polly felt safe and alive.

And terrified.

Chapter Twenty

The community center was on Main Street, just down the sidewalk from Sam's Diner, and the party was in full swing when Polly and Nate walked in. Someone was singing from the stage at the front of the community center. Polly marveled at the town she'd moved to. It was so full of life. As she took a deep breath and walked into the midst of everyone, Nate at her side, she was troubled.

"Would you like some punch?" Nate asked, leaning in toward her so she could hear him over all the laughter, chatter and singing that filled the room.

"That would be nice." Her throat was unusually dry.

Nate squeezed her elbow. "I'll be right back."

Watching him stride through the crowd, she still couldn't believe that she'd, well, she'd agreed to try to *move forward* like this. When she'd awakened this morning, it was not with the thought that today she would agree to try to leave her past behind. Leave Marc behind. Yet she'd done it.

Standing in the midst of the crowd without Nate beside her to muddle her thoughts, she wondered about herself.

She'd had good, valid reasons for not wanting to ever fall in love and remarry. But Nate had stolen past all those reasons and sent her head and heart into a state of confusion. She wasn't even certain if that described what she was feeling. She cared for Nate. There was no denying it. But was that all it was?

She closed her eyes, alone in a sea of people, the variables of her situation swirling around her. Did she love Nate Talbert? The question crowded out everything else. She'd known it was floating around back there, but she'd refused to acknowledge it before. And with good reason.

She didn't want to love him.

So she wouldn't.

"Punch for the lady."

Polly jumped. "Thank you." Her hand trembled as she took the cup.

"You're welcome." Nate sounded happy as he stepped close and rested his hand possessively at the small of her back, sending ripples of awareness along her skin.

Glancing around, she realized that others were noticing how close Nate was standing, and his attentiveness to her. Esther Mae waved with the serving knife she was using to slice the wedding cake, openly beaming with excitement.

Applegate and Stanley were ambling toward them from one direction and Polly saw the speculation in their wizened old eyes. Her instinct was to step back to get away from the questions she knew were coming. What she did instead was step up against Nate, who reacted by sliding his arm around her waist and hugging her to him.

"Careful, there. It'll be okay. They're on our side."

She glanced up at him, and his reassuring smile washed over her. She knew it was true. Still, she felt like she was on a Tilt-A-Whirl. With no protective bar.

"You two lookin' mighty cozy tonight," Applegate said, his voice carrying over the buzz of the room.

"Yup, you two remind me of me and my Elisa Jane. Mighty handsome, if I say so myself."

Deeply touched, Polly smiled and tried to relax, but Nate's arm remained at her waist and he hugged her again. It was meant to reassure her, but it just made her all the more aware of him. He was holding her like she was his to cherish.

"You two clean up nice," Nate said, easily taking the focus away from them as App and Stanley turned to give each other a once-over.

"I look better'n him." Applegate's naturally dower expression brightened with a playful grin.

"You wish," Stanley grunted.

Polly was smiling when Lacy whipped by. "Like I said, cute couple." She winked and was gone, loaded down with dirty dishes on her way through the crowd to the kitchen.

It went on like that all night. Cute little remarks meant to encourage. By the time the evening ended she'd relaxed, helped in part by Nate's steadfast support. As they headed home Polly listened to Gil and Nate talk.

A deep sense of contentment settled over her.

They were halfway home when Gil groaned.

"You okay, pardner?" Nate asked.

Polly turned to look at Gil. He looked a little pale. "Do you feel bad?"

"My stomach is bubbling," he said, and shifted in the seat. "Weddings are sure a good place for cake."

Nate glanced at Polly and grimaced.

Polly frowned at Gil. "So how many pieces did you have?"

"Five, is all. Of the white cake."

"Five!" Polly shook her head. "And the chocolate?"

"Only four." He lay his head back and put his hand on his belly.

"So how's the stomach?" Nate asked, beating Polly.

Gil shrugged. He was starting to look gray. "Aw, that's nothing. I could eat more than that if I wanted."

He didn't sound too convincing, though. By the time they pulled up in the driveway he didn't look good at all. Polly tried to comfort him from the front seat but he was a sick fella. She didn't even state the obvious, hoping he now realized eating nine pieces of cake and no telling how many cups of punch wasn't the best idea.

As soon as they came to a stop Nate hopped out of the truck and eased him into his arms. "I gotcha, pardner." Gil groaned and Polly felt for him. "Hang in there," Nate said, and carried him toward the house. Polly closed the truck door, then jogged ahead and unlocked the front door and held it wide for them.

"This way," she said when Nate stopped at the base of the stairs. Bogie joined them as they hurried to the second floor. She led them into Gil's room and pulled back his covers. In the corner, beneath the sheet, Pepper stirred in his cage but settled down almost instantly.

"I'll get him ready for bed if you want to get him some medicine or something to make him more comfortable," Nate said, his voice hushed.

Polly's heart warmed. "Thank you, I'll be right back."

She hurried down to the kitchen and grabbed a glass of water and the medicine for an upset stomach, then raced back upstairs. Gil and Nat were coming out of the bathroom as she entered Gil's room again. Gil held a wet cloth in his hand and looked pale.

"He should feel a little better," Nate said as he helped him crawl back beneath the covers.

Understanding what that meant, Polly cringed. "I'm so sorry you had to take care of that."

"No problem," Nate said. He moved to the side as Polly filled the spoon with medicine and held it out to Gil. "Take this," she instructed. "It will help. Though I'm pretty sure Nate was right. What just happened in there is going to help the situation immensely."

Gil eyed the spoon and groaned. "I gotta?"

"You gotta."

He heaved a sigh and opened his mouth, resigned to his fate. Polly held in a smile and dutifully stuck the spoon inside. He grimaced as he swallowed, then lay down. "Why does medicine taste so nasty?"

Nate chuckled. "Maybe it's so you'll remember it the next time you decide to eat nine pieces of cake."

Gil looked up at him. "That cake was *goood*."

Polly smoothed his hair off his clammy forehead. "You amaze me, dear. Are you hurting now?"

He shook his head.

"You feel like saying your prayers?"

He nodded and closed his eyes. "Thank you for today. The cake was great. For my daddy. My mom and Nate…" His voice trailed off and Polly continued stroking his hair as he prayed. Now she opened her eyes and was content to watch him fall asleep. In less than a minute his breathing evened out.

"He runs at high speed and then crashes," she whispered, stood and led the way out the door. Bogie had curled up at the foot of his bed and was sleeping, too. He didn't budge when she turned out the light and pulled the door almost shut. Polly wanted to hear Gil if he called.

Nate draped his arm over her shoulders as they walked slowly down the stairs. They were halfway down when she smiled up at him. "That was above and beyond the call of duty. Thank you."

He stopped walking and turned her in his arms. "I know this is going to sound strange, but I enjoyed it."

Polly chuckled. "You're right, it does sound strange." She was standing in the circle of his arms and her face was tilted up so she got a close-up view of his smile. It was devastating from two feet away. From this distance it was a lethal weapon. Coupled with having just gallantly taken care of her son tossing his cookies and not complaining about it, the man was simply irresistible.

"You know I'd do anything for you and Gil."

Polly sighed and lay her head against his powerful chest, taking comfort in the feel of his arms tightening around her. He kissed the top of her head and she sighed.

She believed him.

When she looked up, he seemed to be waiting and their lips were but a breath away from each other's. He waited, as if to give her a chance to turn away. When she didn't, he lowered his lips to hers.

Her knees almost buckled at the tender touch of his lips to hers. When his arms tightened around her, pulling her closer, her blood started pounding in her ears as emotions raged inside her.

"I'm sorry." Polly yanked away, stepping back to clutch the banister. "I can't."

Dan Dawson had come to put new shoes on Taco and Nate's other three horses. Nate had avoided town almost completely the first year after Kayla died. He'd even driven the seventy miles to Ranger for groceries just so he wouldn't have to see the pity in everyone's eyes. His friends had let him know they were there for him, but for the most part they'd given him the space he needed to grieve. He'd started humoring them a bit during the past year in an attempt to squelch the aching loneliness that he'd began to hate and grow weary of.

Dan had been one of the few people who'd seen him

on a regular basis during that entire time. When Nate's horses needed shoes, they needed shoes. And Dan Dawson was the man for the job.

They were friends.

That being the case, Dan was pushing their friendship to the limit.

Nate had been in a foul mood since he'd escorted Pollyanna to Jake's wedding. He was about as wound up as a bull in a squeeze chute.

"So, you going to talk about it? Or you just going to stand there and smolder?" Dan asked as he settled the new shoe on Taco's rear hoof. He'd been working for a while and Nate had known this was coming. Because his head was down Dan didn't see the warning Nate shot his way.

"Nope."

"Come on, man, you cannot tell me you aren't interested in that good-looking woman." He didn't have to say her name for Nate to know who the good-looking woman in question was. He knew everyone in town was talking about him and Pollyanna. Speculating.

Nate ground his jawbone. He had no intention of discussing Pollyanna.

"So that's how it is?" Dan all but cooed.

Nate leaned against the corral and propped his boot behind him on the bottom slat. Better that than kicking it in like he'd contemplated a few times over the past few days.

Dan looked up from his work. "Look, man, when I saw the both of you together at Jake's wedding, I thought maybe things were moving along. That the two of you were an item."

No comment. Nate had thought so, too.

"She'd be good for you."

"How do you know what would be good for me?" Nate exploded, then yanked his hat off and slapped it against his thigh, shooting the other cowboy a warning glare. "Mind your own business, Dan."

Dan was more likely to grow wings. He grinned. "Now, that's more like it. You are alive and well inside that head of yours. Female companionship is good for any man. Giving up a rib was a good idea, if you ask me."

Nate slammed his hat back on and crossed his arms. "Then why aren't you out there pounding the pavement in search of a Mrs. Dawson?"

Completely unaffected by Nate's irritation, Dan shrugged. "Who says I'm not?" He grinned a slow smile, his eyes gleaming with mischief. "If you don't make a move on that neighbor of yours, I figure I'm going to do a little research in that direction myself."

Nate clenched his fist. "The last thing she needs is someone just looking for a little fun." Dan would have to go through him before he let him do anything that might hurt Pollyanna. He'd moved faster than she could accept. He'd been a straight-out fool and been shot out of the saddle because of it.

"I'm insulted, Nate," Dan drawled.

"Yeah, right."

Dan released Taco and straightened. "So I was right. That's how it is."

Nate watched Dan swagger to his tool trailer, his words cutting close. "What's that mean?" he asked, more for Dan's sake than his own. He knew how he felt about Pollyanna. He'd known it since the night after he'd come back from Fort Worth. He'd known it since that night, sitting in Kayla's swing when he'd let her go.

He'd known it sitting on that bench back behind the church that he was in love with Pollyanna McDonald. But she had barely agreed to try to step forward with him. He'd seen it in her eyes. He should have known she wasn't ready to be kissed. Yet foolishly he'd let his brain go out to pasture while he made the mistake of his life.

He hadn't been expecting to fall in love. So he understood her reaction. He'd struggled with it for a few days, even getting irrationally mad at her when she'd fussed over him about his eating habits. But then he'd realized that he could no more deny his love for Pollyanna than he could deny that he'd loved Kayla.

He hadn't expected Gil to get sick. Watching her with Gil, standing in that room, had felt so much like they were a family....

She'd been upset after the kiss and asked him to leave. When he'd called the next day she'd told him that she thought it would be best if they didn't see each other for a while.

When he'd asked what "see each other" meant, she told him there was no easy way to say it but that if he was looking for a new wife she wasn't going to remarry.

Clenching his fist, he struggled with the emotions that stirred anew.

"If you have feelings for her, don't let her go," Dan said.

"Mind your own business," Nate snapped. "And stay away from Pollyanna."

Dan busted out laughing. "Man, you've got it bad. And you can't hide it even if you wanted to."

"Back off, Dan," Nate warned.

"It's been three years. Three years, buddy. Kayla, the Kayla we all loved, isn't here anymore. But you are. It's not going to hurt you to admit you have feelings for someone else."

If he only knew. "That taken from a guy who dates like there's no tomorrow," he goaded, needing someone to take his frustrations out on.

Dan slammed his toolbox shut. "Well, seems to me you, more than most, would know that what time we do have is precious. I like to live, Nate. Maybe it's time you started again. And even if you don't want to, maybe it's time for someone, maybe me if you aren't up for the job, to help that pretty neighbor of yours start living again, too."

Nate took a step toward Dan. They might be friends, but Pollyanna wasn't ready for that kind of pressure. Her reaction to him proved it. "Leave her be, Dan. She doesn't need you dictating to her what living is. And frankly, neither do I." Nate stared at the other man long and hard, certain his message was clear, then he strode toward his house. Madder than he'd been in years.

"You know the way out," he called over his shoulder but didn't look back, even though he knew Dan was still watching him, a big wolfish grin on his face. Who'd Dan Dawson think he was?

Your friend.

Rationally, Nate knew Dan was pushing him because they were friends…but he wasn't thinking rationally at the moment. Hadn't been for a few days now.

Pollyanna had turned his world upside down when he'd knocked on her door to take her to the wedding. Even now, he couldn't stop thinking about how she'd looked at him when she'd opened the door and found him standing there. Pollyanna McDonald had looked at him the way a woman looked at a man, with longing, not the way she would a friend. And in that one look, she'd knocked the breath out of him. He'd felt like he'd hit the ground after being bucked from a wild bronc.

He loved her. And he would move heaven and earth to set Pollyanna's world right.

He just wasn't sure if he could. She'd said all along that she wasn't going to remarry.

And he had a sick feeling that she'd been telling the truth all along. He just hadn't been listening.

Chapter Twenty-One

Sam's was fairly empty as Polly walked through the swinging door. It was just after ten, so it was to be expected that the general population would be out in a pasture somewhere with a bunch of cows instead of sitting inside the diner. She knew it was a busy season for the cowboys, Nate included. It had made avoiding him easier than she'd thought it would over the last week and a half. Avoiding everyone else was a different story.

"Mornin', Pollyanna," Applegate called from his seat at the window where he and Stanley were bent over their morning checkers game.

"Hello, fellas, how's it going this morning?" Holding her head up and smiling, she slipped into a booth to wait on her friends.

"Not so good," Stanley said from beneath bushy eyebrows. "App just beat me."

Applegate snorted and spat a sunflower husk into a spittoon. "He acts like it ain't never happened before."

"It doesn't, you old coot," Stanley grunted, and immediately jumped a couple of App's checkers.

Applegate scowled and scratched his head. "Well, ya didn't have ta be so mean about it."

Polly laughed just as Sam came out from the back. "Thought I heard voices. Other than them two. They're regulars in my head, and I tend ta try 'n' ignore 'em. What kin I do fer ya, young lady?"

"I'm here waiting on your wife and the rest of the gang. I'm just early."

"That's fine. How's about a cup of coffee and maybe some eggs and bacon?"

"Oh, that sounds lovely. You are a man after my own heart."

Grinning, Sam set the cup he was carrying on the table and filled it with dark, rich-smelling coffee. "My heart belongs to another, but I'm purdy certain thar's someone around here who'd be more'n happy to steal yers if ya want him to."

"Yep, we seen you and Nate together at the wedding last week," Applegate said. "Y'all looked right smart together."

"Yep," Stanley said, jumping another checker. "Our Nate, he ain't been one to come out too much on his own, and since you come to town, we're seeing him actually comin' round without somebody draggin' him up."

Polly took a sip of coffee, praying the conversation would go in another direction. But obviously the good Lord had other plans, because Applegate jumped a checker then turned suddenly serious eyes on her.

"Take it from me, little darlin', you're too young to be sittin' around out thar at yor house all alone. And the same goes for Nate. I lost my sweet Birdie six years ago, and thar ain't a day goes by that I don't miss her. But the Lord gave us many a good year together. It was a good life. Now, take you and Nate…"

Polly just wished someone would shoot her now. But she couldn't really be too upset. After all, Applegate had lost his wife. He knew.

"You two are young'uns. You both need to be lookin' out fer someone new to share yer life with."

"App's right. My Elisa Jane' she and me had forty-two years, six months and two days together," Stanley said. "Twern't long enough by my way of thankin', but them's the breaks. I was blessed to get what I got. Now I'm left sitting here across from App's ugly mug whuppin' him at checkers every day. 'Course, I don't know what I done to rile the good Lord bad enough to give me this punishment." He spat a husk into the spittoon and grinned. "The thang is, you and Nate, y'all got a whole life ahead of you. And then thar's the boy. He needs a dad."

She'd entered the twilight zone. *Please, Lord, have mercy and save me from this.*

"You know Nate. He took it really bad when his wife died. It was a sorrowful thing watching that spunky little gal wilt like she did."

"That cancer, it ain't a respecter of nobody. Young, old, it don't matter. Our boy Nate's a good man who deserves a second chance for happiness," Applegate said, rubbing his jaw. "He was blest ta have a good woman once. Which means it ain't just any woman that will do this go-around." Applegate's thin face drooped into a deep frown as he looked at Polly. "It'll take someone special. Like you."

She wanted to crawl under the table. Instead, she clutched the hot coffee cup and prayed hard that the Lord would calm her. She'd worked herself to the bone over the past week. It had been good for the bed-and-breakfast because she was basically ready to open, and all because she'd been trying to avoid thinking about Nate. Or Marc! Her heart had suddenly become a jigsaw puzzle tossed into the air and now lay scrambled at her feet.

When Nate had kissed her…emotions she'd thought she could only ever feel for Marc had come to life. She hadn't known what to do with them or how to handle them. She still didn't.

She'd been avoiding Nate ever since. Gil, however, had gone over to see him almost every day. Returning to the house hours later percolating with stories of what he and Nate had done together. There was no escaping that Gil had given his heart over to Nate Talbert, totally and completely.

Before she had a chance to think more about it, Sam brought out her plate of eggs and the diner door swung open and the ladies burst into the room, Esther Mae in the lead.

"I tell you it'll be a really interesting twist or a pure disaster," she was saying.

"True, but if it's a disaster it'll be interesting. Howdy, Pollyanna," Norma Sue sang out, sounding like Minnie Pearl.

Greetings were volleyed from all directions as Norma Sue slid into the booth beside Polly. Esther Mae slid into the bench across from her, leaving room for Adela. She detoured to the back to see Sam while Lacy grabbed a chair and turned it around so she could face everyone. Sheri trailed in behind them, her fancy cowgirl boots clunking on the hardwood floor as she grabbed the chair beside Lacy.

Applegate and Stanley seemed to lean out from their checker game, almost as if they were joining in on the meeting from across the room.

"So let's talk more about the new addition to the festival. Pollyanna, what's your take on this bike situation?"

All eyes turned to Polly. "The bike situation?"

"Yes," Esther Mae said, her eyes bright from barely contained excitement. "It's your idea, after all. So we thought you could be in charge of getting it going."

"You can do that, can't you?" Lacy said. "I would, but I have my hands pretty full already. We've been tossing the idea around ever since you brought it up. The girls bring their bikes…and maybe we can have like a drawing of some sort to figure out who races with whom." She gasped suddenly and clapped her hands. "Auction! We could have a bachelor auction to see who rides bikes together."

"Or…" Sheri interjected, her tone dry as usual. "Here's an idea. Maybe we could just let people team up on their own. I bet they could do it."

Lacy whacked her on the arm with a rolled-up napkin. "Har-har." She laughed.

Polly hoped Sheri's idea stuck. She'd only mentioned the bike race and now they were all expecting her to elaborate.

"Are the men going to ride the women on the handlebars?" Esther Mae asked. "You know my Hank and I used to do that."

Norma Sue's mouth dropped open. "How'd you get up on those handlebars? I know Hank didn't lift you up there. Maybe with a crane."

Esther Mae harrumphed indignantly. "My Hank could if he'd wanted to."

"Yeah, but the question is if he wanted to." Norma Sue grinned, her smile wide at her wit, while Esther Mae looked equally perturbed by it.

Lacy chuckled, waving her hands. "Okay, you two, cut it out. Poor Pollyanna's going to think y'all are serious."

Esther Mae harrumphed again. "And what makes you think we aren't? My Hank could pick me up and set me on those handlebars if he wanted to. I only climbed on a chair to get up there because I didn't want him to hurt his back."

Norma Sue coughed and looked down at her butterball figure. "It's okay, Esther. I was only teasing you. Even if I'd been able to climb onto the handlebars by myself, my poor Roy Don wouldn't have been able to hold the bike up under this weight. Even with help!"

"Now, that paints some picture, Norma Sue." Sheri laughed.

"Don't it, though," Norma Sue chortled huskily.

"That man loves me, though, and he'd try if I asked him." She looked at Pollyanna. "And you know that's all that counts."

Pollyanna smiled with a mixture of relief and respect. She was glad she'd moved to Mule Hollow and had these dear women to be around. They were funny, and fun, and yet there was love here. She envied them their long and happy marriages. She thought of Marc and missed him so. Nate moved into her thoughts and Marc faded to black. The very idea caused her to lose her breath.

"I could hear you girls all the way in the kitchen," Adela said, sitting primly down beside Esther Mae.

Adela was also a widow. It hit Polly that maybe Adela would understand these emotions that were tearing her apart. Maybe she needed to talk with her. Maybe she could help her understand what was wrong with her. Because despite trying to avoid it, there was no denying that she needed help.

She'd avoided Nate, but avoiding all the troubled thoughts churning around inside her head was a little harder to accomplish with each passing day. She needed to talk to someone. And though she'd been praying, God had been silent.

She realized as she looked around the room that maybe the Lord hadn't been silent after all. Maybe he'd just been waiting for her to utilize the help He'd already given her.

Nate had a load of feed to pick up at Pete's Feed and Seed and decided to swing by there on his way home from the cattle auction. He'd had a flat on the way in and had had a time changing the tire. He was tired and dusty as he backed his truck up to the loading dock. When he looked up, the last person he expected to see was Pollyanna coming out of Sam's.

His heart started thundering automatically at the sight of her. By the look on her face when she saw him, he was the last person she'd wanted to run into.

He'd almost had her agreeing to ease their relationship to a notch above friendship and then he'd gone and rushed her. Made her as skittish as a colt after a bad fall.

After all she'd said how she hated cowboys flirting with her...if she hated that, then she'd sure hate to hear one had fallen in love with her.

"Hi," she said, stopping a couple of feet in front of him. She had her hair loose today, no ties or ribbons holding it back, and the breeze caused it to flutter around her face. She looked tired. Lovely, but tired.

She wasn't sleeping. It didn't take a detective to figure it out, but he also had a spy. Gil had told him that his mom had been working at night. Nate translated that as she wasn't sleeping. He'd also told Nate that she'd cried two nights ago. Nate's gut constricted when he thought about her crying alone behind closed doors. He'd caused this.

But he'd tried to help Gil. They'd talked a long time yesterday as they'd fed cows. Nate had felt like he'd been able to relieve the boy's worries some. He'd made certain that Gil understood that he could always come to him with any worries or problems. But he wasn't so sure Pollyanna would want to know that Gil was so worried about her.

"Hi," he said lamely.

"Hello."

She threaded her fingers absently through her hair. Nate wished he were the one doing that. *Like she'd welcome that, cowboy.*

"Gil said you and he had a long talk yesterday."

Nate's antennae went up. "Yes, we did," he said cautiously. How much of their conversation did Gil tell her about? "How are you feeling?" he asked, wondering if she would open up to him like she used to.

Her gaze skittered away from him down Main Street. "Fine. Look, about the other night."

"I'm sorry," he said. "I didn't mean to kiss you. To rush you like that. We've both stepped out on black ice here." He hoped that eased her mind some. Maybe set them back on firmer ground. Gave him somewhere to build a new foundation from.

She nodded and took a deep breath. "I know. Did you hear," she said suddenly, "I'm heading up the bike race at the fair day." She smiled too brightly.

He smiled back, glad to get a smile any way he could. "How'd you get roped into that?"

"Well, you and I did inspire it. And honestly, did I really have a choice after the ladies decided for me?" She smiled again, and this time it was relaxed and real. It instantly transformed the mood.

"I see what you mean," Nate said, seeing a ray of sunshine and a moment of opportunity that he wasn't about to pass up. If the Lord was giving him a heads-up on all his prayers, he wasn't about to pass it up. "That's going to be a ton of work. And the clock is ticking down fast." That was an understatement. The ladies had put out the word and called everyone to get ready to work. Next weekend all the decorating would start and it would go on all week until vendors started showing up. The place would be packed because Mule Hollow's calendar of fun events was a hit with the ladies and also with families and other tourists. At least, he'd heard everyone talk about them. He as of yet hadn't actually attended any of them.

"So. Since me and my white legs were part of the inspiration to all of this, could you use some help?" He was pushing, and praying that she'd relax and get comfortable with him again.

"You mean you'd be willing to do a little suntanning in order to prevent major wipeouts on the road as you ride by?" she asked, her lips curving gently upward.

How was it that a simple smile could make his world tilt back into place?

"Cute," he said, while he felt like yelling out a big thank-you to the good Lord. "I'd do that and more for you."

A shadow dimmed her eyes and her lips flattened as they studied each other. *Way to go, Nate. You couldn't leave it be.* She looked fragile and brave all mixed in together. His heart longed for her happiness.

"You're going to be okay, Pollyanna McDonald."

She blinked, her eyes suddenly bright with moisture and nodded. "Friends?"

He nodded. "Always."

"Gotta go," she said softly, backing up, looking winsome and sad at the same time.

Watching her walk down Main Street, Nate said another prayer that whatever the Lord's plan was for them, that He'd be sure to let him in on it soon.

Chapter Twenty-Two

It was late, eleven o'clock, and all the house was sleeping when Polly finished working in her office. "And that does it," she said, pressing Send on the e-mail to confirm her last available opening for the weekend of the festival. The official opening of her bed-and-breakfast was nearly here.

It was a satisfying feeling to know that with God's help she'd accomplished what she'd set out to do when she'd moved to Mule Hollow.

Satisfying...gratifying...rewarding, all were words she could use to describe the sense that opening the business gave her.

She ran her hand across the edge of her desk and glanced at the phone, then up to the photo of her, Gil and Marc. She blinked hard as her gaze fell once more to the phone.

Her fingers tapped restlessly.

Anxious and unsettled, she stood and moved to turn

out the lights. Closing the door, she stood in her newly painted hallway. She'd wanted to call Nate and tell him she was booked. She wandered up the stairs, through the sleeping house.

She couldn't sleep. Hadn't in days.

Passing her bedroom door, she continued on to the third story, past the row of small bookcases and the cozy reading nook she'd created, and out onto the tiny balcony where she settled into the cushy bench seat. She'd found the bench in the attic. It was perfect for the space, allowing for one or two people to sit and watch the stars together. Tonight she pulled her knees up and wrapped her arms around them tightly. Needing to hug something.

Since Marc's death, she'd missed the feel of his arms around her. She'd missed sharing her day. Her life.

Was this the way her life would play out from here on out? She'd spent many nights in their old home sitting on the deck looking up at the night sky. It was as if at least in the dark of the night, when the silence of the house was too much, she found solace beneath the stars.

She cast out her weary, heavy, laden heart, looking to feel connected. God was up there, looking down on her, and He cared.

Polly had finally gone to talk with Adela about the conflicted emotions warring inside of her. She'd helped some, told her she needed to move on, but not to rush it. That when the time was right for her to love again she would know it.

That she didn't need to be afraid of it.

Adela had known immediately that Polly was afraid.

Polly was afraid of Nate.

He was a wonderful man. He was great with her son, he was kind, thoughtful and warm…he was a man of honor. He loved the Lord, though he'd also suffered great loss. The list could go on and on. He was the kind of man that any woman couldn't help falling in love with….

She hadn't come to Mule Hollow looking for love.

But you've found it.

She buried her head in her hands and drew in a few slow breaths. Easy. Easy.

She'd been in love.

Lifting her head, a flash of light caught her eye and she realized it was headlights coming down Nate's drive. She was startled to see a vehicle at this late hour and watched as it followed his drive and turned out onto the road. In the moonlight she could clearly see that it was Nate's truck. Coming her direction. When he turned and started up her drive, she sprang to her feet.

Shocked and a little alarmed, she hurried inside the house and down the stairs. At the second floor she stubbed her toe and made enough noise to wake Gil. She paused, holding her toe and waited. When she didn't hear him stirring she continued down the stairs. Had something happened? Was there an emergency? It was so late, that surely he needed help of some sort. She was her mother's child and believed telephone calls or knocks on the front door after ten meant bad news. After twelve meant really bad news.

Of course, thank goodness, it wasn't always the case, but tell that to her pounding heart and sick stomach.

By the time she got the door opened and stepped out onto the porch, Nate was storming up the path.

Her heart lurched into her throat. "Nate, what's the matter?" she asked, hurrying toward him. The look in his eyes stopped her in her tracks on the edge of the porch.

"Pollyanna, we need to talk," he snarled, looking like he could take on an army in hand-to-hand combat if needed.

She wasn't going to argue with that. "Okay," she said. She'd never seen him this way. There was fire in his eyes as he studied her. And he was a mess, she realized. His hat was missing, his dark hair was tousled as if he'd raked his hands through it repeatedly, or scrubbed it one good time like a washboard, leaving the waves as wild as the look in his eyes. As distraught as the look in his eyes.

Instantly her need to comfort him sprang forward and she wanted to smooth away the furrows between his eyes. To offer words of comfort, to hold him close as she longed to be held by him…she longed for him. None of these thoughts surprised her. It was part of why she'd been unable to sleep. One of the reasons she'd gone to talk to Adela.

Nate Talbert made her think about being a woman again.

He made her pulse skip and her heart race.

He made her feel alive again.

No man other than Marc had ever made her long to be held. Long to be kissed… She'd struggled with the feelings he'd awakened in her when he'd held her and when he'd kissed her. It had been brief, yet it made her long for more. It had scared her so.

"What's wrong?" she asked. "Has something happened?"

He raked his hands through his hair...then in the same movement let his hands fall to his sides, balled into fists.

"I value you," he said.

Not exactly what she'd expected. "I value you, too," she said, realizing in her heart it wasn't exactly what she'd been hoping he'd say. The realization hit her hard. All the feelings she had for him, the feelings that were causing her such turmoil fought for acknowledgment.

"What I mean is, in the short while since you moved here, I've been able to talk to you like I haven't talked to anyone since Kayla."

So that was it. "I feel the same way," she said, trying to ignore the disappointment surging through her even as she spoke the truth. "We have a bond because of Kayla and Marc. I understand." And she did, she didn't want more than that. No, that wasn't it, either. Looking at him, she knew it was that she didn't want to *want* more than that.

"No." His tone startled her. "I'm not certain you do. I'm sorry, I didn't mean for it to happen, but it has. I know that you hate it. You said so yourself, but I've fought it and it's no use."

Polly's temple started throbbing. "What's happened?"

He let his gaze drop to the newly budded tulips before locking with hers again. "I'm tired of sitting over there at my house all alone, Pollyanna. I'm tired of swinging in my swing thinking about all the things I wanted with Kayla and knowing I'm never going to have any of it. I'm tired of looking at my life like it's a long black road that goes nowhere. And that's exactly how I've felt since Kayla breathed her last breath in my arms. I'm tired of my arms being empty."

Polly took a step back, purely out of reflex as his words, similar to her own, sank into her heart.

He took a deep breath. "I'm sorry, Pollyanna. I know it's crazy for me to be on your doorstep in the dead of night, but I've been thinking about this for days and it's got to be said. I love you, Pollyanna."

She stiffened and looked at the ground.

"Believe me, I wasn't expecting this. But it's happened and I know you aren't looking for anything more than what you had with Marc. And I know you hate cowboys flirting with you. And believe me, I'm telling you this so that you'll... Honestly I haven't a clue why I'm telling you this." The look he gave her was helpless.

That made her laugh. It surprised her, it came so quickly. Like a punch line from a joke that hadn't seemed funny at first, and then snuck up on you and made you laugh.

But he looked so apologetic and confused, and honestly she knew exactly where he was coming from. She was living in her own state of confusion. Battling emotions she didn't know what to do with.

"That wasn't entirely true," he said. Stepping up onto the step below her, he reached across the distance she'd put between them, cupped her elbow and tugged her close so they were eye to eye.

Polly's blood was a turbulent river in her ears, the power making her dizzy. Part of her wanted to run while part of her wanted to stay.

"I value you," he repeated softly. "I value our ability to talk, I value the friendship." He smiled and touched her cheek, running his thumb slowly along her jawline. "I'm not expecting you to feel anything for me. The last thing I want is to pressure you. But I think you do feel more for me. And I think I scared you off the other night when I kissed you."

His tenderness drew her and Polly lifted her hands, giving into the need to touch him. Her fingers trembled as she placed her palms on the sides of his face and simply held them there as emotions collided within her.

Nate stood still as if he thought if he moved she'd pull away. But his emotions were open and clear in his eyes as he drank her in with them. Marc had looked at her like that, and thinking of him brought tears to her own eyes.

The moment Nate saw the tears brimming, his hands came up to cup her face. "Pollyanna, please don't cry. I know you love Marc. I know you're not looking to fall in love again. And if God would grant me one wish I would give Marc back to you just to see you happy."

Wrapping her in his embrace, he stepped up onto the porch beside her. Her hands slid to his chest as he pulled her close and held her. And in the still of the night, for a brief moment, with her hands and her cheek resting on Nate's broad chest, his heartbeat melding with her own, she felt the tide recede. The turmoil eased and she was able to rest in a place as smooth as the flawless sand left in the ocean's wake. For a moment she was able to forget everything and see the promise of a new beginning…if she wanted it. If she could just trust.

She pulled away, uncertain. "I didn't come here for this."

"I know," he said, holding her at arm's length when she would have pulled away. "But you were the answer to my prayers. You and Gil. I started waking up looking forward to my day almost immediately after meeting you." He gave a lopsided grin that made her heart smile. "You were so cute all dripping wet and so upset with yourself for not being able to handle the leak by yourself. Miss Independent."

Polly backed out of Nate's arms. "I wanted so much to make it on my own. To make Marc proud."

"I'm sure he is. You're doing great, Pollyanna. But you have to start living life for yourself. You can't keep doing everything to make Marc happy. You have to make yourself happy. And Gil."

Nate walked to the porch railing. Placing his hands on it, he leaned into them, staring up at the sky. "I know it makes you feel guilty. Thinking like that makes me feel guilty, too. But that's the way it is."

His words stung. But she knew they were right. But knowing it didn't make it any better.

"Gil is a great kid, Marc would be proud of him. I feel like I'm stealing his blessings when I'm with Gil…when I'm with you. But, Pollyanna, Marc isn't here and I want to be there for Gil. And for you."

Polly couldn't speak. Didn't know what to say. But she wanted him there, too.

"No strings attached, if that's the way you want it."

Is that what she wanted? "Nate, that wouldn't work."

Her heart was thundering, as Nate sat on the edge of the railing and pulled her to stand in front of him. Lifting her chin with his finger, he searched her eyes with his. "Kayla is as much a part of me as Marc is of you. But I want you and Gil in my life. It's as simple as that. And I'm willing to give us both the time that we need to adjust to the idea. I tried to say that at the church that night. Then I rushed you. But I'm here to stay, Pollyanna, and unless you tell me there's not a chance that you could ever love me then I'm not going away."

Pulling her close, he wrapped his arms around her. Polly stiffened, trying to make sense of her feelings. What did she want? His words were noble and flattering, even. This wonderful man was telling her that he wanted her in his life…that he was tired of being alone. That he'd fallen for her and that he was willing to wait for as long as it took for her to get comfortable with the idea. She could see his chest lifting as if his heart was pounding as maliciously as hers.

"Nate," she whispered. "Kiss me again."

He went still. "Are you sure?"

She nodded. "I need you to kiss me."

His gaze darkened in the moonlight. And then he lowered his head and touched his lips to hers.

It was the merest of touches and yet it flowed through her. A hailstorm of emotions hit her all at once. Until Nate first kissed her, Marc's kisses had been the only ones she'd known from the first moment she'd lain eyes on him. She'd never thought she'd ever want or need anyone else.

But she knew now that wasn't true. Lifting trembling hands, she wrapped them around Nate's neck and pulled him close as tears slipped from her eyes and the band around her heart broke.

"I love you, Nate. It scares me, but it's true."

The words came out, halting the kiss, exposing her heart. She felt a freedom in saying the words.

"Pollyanna," Nate whispered against her cheek, his strong arms holding her tighter. "I didn't expect—"

"Nate," she said, leaning back to look into his eyes, "I've been fighting the growing feelings I have for you from almost the first moment we met. I'm not saying it's going to be easy. But I've been sitting here night after night fighting letting go. I thought holding on to Marc would make me happy, but…but it hasn't. I'm understanding that if I hold too tightly to the past I can never be content. And I know that not acknowledging my love for you isn't making me happy, either."

"Sounds like you have a problem."

She smiled. "No. A very wise man used to tell me over and over again that life is for the living." Polly felt tears as she glanced at Marc's tulips, the bright, perfect yellow blooms open and full with promise. "I love you, Nate Talbert. I loved Marc. I always will, just as you loved Kayla…but I feel them smiling right now. For the first time in so long, I feel peace."

Nate's eyes grew bright as he nodded and Polly felt joy bright and strong spill across her heart.

"I love you, Pollyanna McDonald, and I love Gil as if he was my own. And I promise to love and cherish you, and I make that vow before God, and to Marc's memory. I will always be here for you both as long as God gives me breath to breathe. Will you marry me?"

Polly wiped tears from her eyes and wrapped her arms around his neck, pulling his forehead down to meet hers. "Yes," she said, and then she kissed him.

And inside from behind the curtain where he and Bogie had been watching and praying, Gilbert Marcus McDonald did a happy dance.

Chapter Twenty-Three

The town was crowded as Pollyanna stood at the sign-up booth for the First Annual Mule Hollow Cowboy Bike Race. It was a five-mile race along a route she and Nate had mapped out. It was a mixture of smooth paved roads and rough dirt roads—they'd decided to mix it up a bit and see how the couples fared. Of course, she and Nate had already tested it out and had had a blast figuring out how to get from the starting line to finish line. Like Esther Mae had suggested, they'd made it a couples' race with one bike. And though they were drawing names out of a hat so that the partners were a surprise, they were leaving it up to the couples to decide exactly how to get the bike across the finish line. They could choose for one to pedal while one rode on the handlebars, the seat or the cross bar...or if need be one could run or walk along beside the bike. The only rule to this bike race was that it was a single guy, a single gal and a bike. And a road that represented the good, easy times of life and the rough hardships that came along, too. The couples had creative choice on how to succeed.

All the teams had been determined and Polly's part in the race was done. As she set her pencil down, Nate came up behind her and put his arms around her. They'd been through good times and they'd lived through hardships…and now they were starting a new life together. Polly leaned her head back and rested it against his chest.

"Hello, stranger," she said, planting a kiss at the base of his neck. She loved this man so much. In the week since they'd faced the fact that they loved each other she'd felt such a peace. She knew that she could have made it on her own, that she was strong enough to have made her life here in Mule Hollow enjoyable and fulfilling. Though she'd lived through the loss of her beloved Marc, God had fulfilled the verse that she'd read that morning in the Book of Psalms: *The Lord is my strength and song, and is become my salvation.* And it had been true, God had never left her as she'd gone on with her life. He'd been her strength and her song when she was weak. And he'd been her salvation in the worst of times. She would have been okay, but God had brought her to Nate for a reason.

She felt blessed that He'd given her a new love so remarkable, so unexpected. She didn't know what the future held for them, but she knew that she was excited to live it and find out as they went.

"Hello, yourself," Nate said into her ear. "So how'd the pairing off go over?" he asked, snuggling close.

"Oh, if Norma Sue and Esther Mae wanted sparks, well, there they are." She nodded down the way a bit to where Dan Dawson stood grinning cockily at Ashby Templeton. Ashby, looking less than thrilled that Norma Sue had pulled their names out of the hat and teamed them up, had her arms crossed, a frown on her face and fire flashing in her usually composed eyes.

Nate chuckled and pulled Polly close, nuzzling her neck. "That right there ought to be interesting. You smell delicious," he said, sounding distracted.

Polly chuckled and turned into his arms. "If they make it back in one piece they might actually find out those sparks they're sending off could fuel a lifetime of love. I'm so happy. Did I tell you how happy I am? And I hope there are a whole lot of these couples who find what we have." Polly cupped Nate's chin. "So is everything set?"

"Everything is set. Lacy's about to make the announcement. Are you sure this is the way you want to do it?"

Polly smiled warmly all the way from her heart. "Positive. I don't want to waste another moment. Is Gil ready?"

"He and Bogie are waiting. He's so happy," Nate's voice caught and his eyes, so intense, seemed to look into Polly's very soul. "Pollyanna, do you know how blessed I feel?"

"I feel the same way."

"Hello, everyone, y'all come gather around, please," Lacy said over the microphone that had been set up at the platform in the center of Main Street.

"We are so glad for this tremendous turnout for our Mule Hollow Fair day. Before we get the fun under way, though, we have an awesome surprise in store for everyone. *We're having a wedding!*"

Nate grinned and kissed Polly soundly on the lips as whoops erupted from cowboys throughout the crowd. "Are you ready to be my bride?" he whispered, stepping back and holding out his hand.

Polly looked from Nate toward the platform where a beaming Gil and Bogie waited beside Pastor Lewis and Lacy. Polly had never been more ready for anything in her life.

Life is for living, babe.

"Oh, yes. I'm *sooo* ready," she said, and placed her hand in Nate's, her heart bursting with love when he smiled down at her. Then, hand in hand, they walked through the crowd toward their new beginning. Along the way people called out their good wishes, smiling and whooping with joy for them.

And somewhere on the gentle breeze Polly heard a familiar soft whisper from her past… *"Catch ya later, gator. Have a beautiful life."*

And looking up at Nate, Polly knew she would.

* * * * *

Dear Reader,

I am so pleased you've chosen to spend time in Mule Hollow! I had many hopes as I wrote this book, as you will read below.

I hope this story blesses you as much as it blessed me. As a fairly young widow myself, *Next Door Daddy* was born straight from my heart. My heart's desire was to tell a story that not only gave hope of falling in love again after having loved once, but most of all to celebrate and pay tribute to how one's love lives on in the lives of those left behind. My hope is that I've done so. Pollyanna McDonald, her darling son, Gil, and her wonderful menagerie of crazy animals gave me the perfect way to do just that!

I hope as you read Pollyanna and Nate's love story that it prompts a warm and beautiful memory of someone you've loved. I hope it makes you smile and I pray it gives you joy and renewed strength.

And last but most importantly, I pray each of you knows how wonderful and gracious God is. His love is everlasting. He is with us in the best of times, but more importantly, He is with us in the worst of times. When we are weak, He is strong. If you are grieving, if you are hurting in any way, I pray that God surrounds you with His love and comfort and that in His arms you find peace.

I love hearing from readers, and try my hardest to respond. You can reach me through my Web site, www.debraclopton.com, or at P.O. Box 1125, Madisonville, Texas 77864, or through Steeple Hill's address.

Until next time love, laugh for the joy of it and hug those you can!

Debra Clopton

P.S. I hope you'll come back to Mule Hollow in June for *Her Baby Dreams,* when Ashby Templeton and Dan Dawson keep the sparks flying!

QUESTIONS FOR DISCUSSION

1. Did you enjoy *Next Door Daddy?* What was your favorite moment?

2. If you've lost someone you love, please share with everyone a special memory of them that makes you happy.

3. In *Next Door Daddy,* how important was it for Pollyanna to keep Gil's father's memory alive? Why?

4. Since they were both Christians, were you surprised that Pollyanna and Nate had trouble going back to church? Have you or someone you know experienced this or something similar? What helped you or them?

5. Nate and Pollyanna both finally realized they could glean comfort and insight from the ones around them who'd already lost a spouse. What does the Bible say about this? Why did it take them so long to think about reaching out?

6. Because she'd felt so blessed during her life with Marc, Pollyanna felt guilty for missing her old life. Can you understand this reasoning? Do you think she was dishonoring God by not being content with her new life?

7. Marc believed life is for the living. What about you? Not that you have to go to the extremes of skydiving, but in what ways could you live life more abundantly? Would you give more time to the Lord? More time to your family? Laugh more? Help someone in need? Go skydiving?

8. How important is it to keep in contact with someone who is grieving? How could you minister to someone like Nate who needs time alone? Did the residents of Mule Hollow do this right?

9. After the death of a spouse one can feel displaced, as Nate and Pollyanna both felt. What can you as a friend and the church do to help this?

10. Did this book make you want to hug the ones you love and cherish them while you are blessed to have them? I hope it did that and I also hope it helped you celebrate the lives of the ones who've gone before us.

*Powerful, engaging stories of romance, adventure
and faith set in the past—when life was simpler
and faith played a major role in everyday lives.*

Turn the page for a sneak preview of
THE BRITON
By
Catherine Palmer

*Love Inspired Historical—love and faith
throughout the ages.
A brand-new line from Steeple Hill Books.
Launching this February!*

"Welcome to the family, Briton," said one of Olaf's men in a mocking voice. "We look forward to the presence of a woman at our hall."

Bronwen grasped her tunic and yanked it from the Viking's thick fingers. As she stepped away from the table, she heard the drunken laughter of the barbarians behind her. How could her father have betrothed her to the old Viking?

Running down the stone steps toward the heavy oak door that led outside the keep, Bronwen gathered her mantle about her. She ordered the doorman to open it, and he did so reluctantly, pressing her to carry a torch. But Bronwen pushed past him and fled into the darkness.

Dashing down the steep, pebbled hill toward the beach, she felt the frozen ground give way to sand. She threw off her veil and circlet and kicked away her shoes.

Racing alongside the pounding surf, she felt hot tears of anger and shame well up and stream down her cheeks. With no concern for her safety, Bronwen ran and ran, her long braids streaming behind her, falling loose, drifting like a tattered black flag.

Blinded with weeping, she did not see the dark form that loomed suddenly in her path and stopped dead her headlong sprint. Bronwen shrieked in surprise and fear as iron arms pinned her, and a heavy cloak threatened to suffocate her.

"Release me!" she cried. "Guard! Guard, help me!"

"Hush, my lady." A deep voice emanated from the darkness. "I mean you no harm. What demon drives you to run so madly in the night without fear for your safety?"

"Release me, villain! I am the daughter—"

"I shall hold you until you calm yourself. We had heard there were witches in Amounderness, but I had not thought to meet one so openly."

Still held tight in the man's arms, Bronwen drew back and peered up at the hooded figure. "You! You are the man who spied on our feast. Release me at once, or I shall call the guard upon you."

The man chuckled at this and turned toward his companions, who stood in a group nearby. Bronwen caught hold of the back of his hood and jerked it down to reveal a head of glossy raven curls. But the man's face was shrouded in darkness yet, and as he looked at her, she could not read his expression.

"So you are the blessed bride-to-be." He pulled the hood back over his head. "Your father has paired you with an interesting choice."

Relieved that her captor did not appear to be a high-wayman, she sagged from his warm hands onto the wet sand. "Please leave me here alone. I need peace to think. Go on your way."

The tall stranger shrugged off his outer mantle and wrapped it around her shoulders. "Why did your father betroth you thus to the aged Viking?" he asked.

"For one purported to be a spy, you know precious little about Amounderness. But I shall tell you, as it is all common knowledge."

She pulled the cloak tightly about her, reveling in its warmth. "Our land, Amounderness, once was Briton territory. Olaf Lothbrok, my betrothed, came here as a youth when the Viking invasions had nearly subsided. He took the lands directly to the south of Rossall Hall from their Briton lord. Then, of course, the Normans came, and Amounderness was pillaged by William the Conqueror's army."

The man squatted on the sand beside Bronwen. He listened with obvious interest as she continued with the familiar tale. "When William took an account of Amounderness in his Domesday Book, he recorded no remaining lords and few people at all. But he did not know the Britons. Slowly, we crept out of hiding and returned to our halls. My father's family reoccupied Rossall Hall. And there we live, as we should, watching over our serfs as they fish and grow their meager crops. Indeed, there is not much here for the greedy Normans to want, if they are the ones for whom you spy."

Unwilling to continue speaking when her heart was so heavy, Bronwen stood and turned toward the sea. The traveler rose beside her and touched her arm.

"Olaf Lothbrok's lands—together with your father's—will reunite most of Amounderness. A clever plan. Your sister's future husband holds the rest of the adjoining lands, I understand."

"You've done your work, sir. Your lord will be pleased. Who is he—some land-hungry Scottish baron? Or have you forgotten that King Stephen gave Amounderness to the Scots as a trade for their support in his war with Matilda? I certainly hope your lord is not a Norman. He would be so disappointed to learn he has no legal rights here. Now, if you will excuse me?"

Bronwen turned and began walking back along the beach toward Rossall Hall. She felt better for her run, and somehow her father's plan did not seem so far-fetched anymore. Distant lights twinkled through the fog that was rolling in from the west, and she suddenly realized what a long way she had come.

"My lady," the stranger's voice called out from behind her.

Bronwen kept walking, unwilling to face again the one who had seen her in her humiliation. She did not care what he reported to his master.

"My lady, you have a bit of a walk ahead of you." The traveler strode forward to join her. "Perhaps I should accompany you to your destination."

"You leave me no choice, I see."

"I am not one to compromise myself, dear lady. I follow the path God has set before me and none other."

"And just who are you?"

"I am called Jacques."

"French. A Norman, as I suspected."

The man chuckled. "Not nearly as Norman as you are Briton."

As they approached the fortress, Bronwen could see that the guests had not yet begun to disperse. Perhaps no one had missed her, and she could slip quietly into bed beside her sister, Gildan.

She turned to go, but he took her arm and studied her face in the moonlight. Then, gently, he drew her into the folds of his hooded cloak. "Perhaps the bride would like the memory of a younger man's embrace to warm her," he whispered.

Astonished, Bronwen attempted to remove his arms from around her waist. But she could not escape his lips as they found her own. The kiss was soft and warm, melting away her resistance like the sun upon the snow. Before she had time to react, he was striding back down the beach.

Bronwen stood stunned for a moment, clutching his woolen mantle about her. Suddenly she cried out, "Wait, Jacques! Your mantle!"

The dark one turned to her. "Keep it for now," he shouted into the wind. "I shall ask for it when we meet again."

* * * * *

Don't miss this deeply moving
Love Inspired Historical story about
a medieval lady who finds strength in
God to save her family legacy—and to
open her heart to love.

THE BRITON
by Catherine Palmer
available February 2008.

And also look for
HOMESPUN BRIDE
by Jillian Hart
where a Montana woman discovers that
love is the greatest blessing of all.

REQUEST YOUR FREE BOOKS!

2 FREE INSPIRATIONAL NOVELS
PLUS 2
FREE
MYSTERY GIFTS

YES! Please send me 2 FREE Love Inspired® novels and my 2 FREE mystery gifts. After receiving them, if I don't wish to receive any more books, I can return the shipping statement marked "cancel." If I don't cancel, I will receive 4 brand-new novels every month and be billed just $3.99 per book in the U.S., or $4.74 per book in Canada, plus 25¢ shipping and handling per book and applicable taxes, if any*. That's a savings of 20% off the cover price! I understand that accepting the 2 free books and gifts places me under no obligation to buy anything. I can always return a shipment and cancel at any time. Even if I never buy another book from Steeple Hill, the two free books and gifts are mine to keep forever.

113 IDN EF26   313 IDN EF27

Name	(PLEASE PRINT)	
Address		Apt. #
City	State/Prov.	Zip/Postal Code

Signature (if under 18, a parent or guardian must sign)

Order online at www.LoveInspiredBooks.com

Or mail to Steeple Hill Reader Service™:

IN U.S.A.: P.O. Box 1867, Buffalo, NY 14240-1867
IN CANADA: P.O. Box 609, Fort Erie, Ontario L2A 5X3

Not valid to current Love Inspired subscribers.

Want to try two free books from another series?
Call 1-800-873-8635 or visit www.morefreebooks.com

* Terms and prices subject to change without notice. NY residents add applicable sales tax. Canadian residents will be charged applicable provincial taxes and GST. This offer is limited to one order per household. All orders subject to approval. Credit or debit balances in a customer's account(s) may be offset by any other outstanding balance owed by or to the customer. Please allow 4 to 6 weeks for delivery.

Your Privacy: Steeple Hill is committed to protecting your privacy. Our Privacy Policy is available online at www.eHarlequin.com or upon request from the Reader Service. From time to time we make our lists of customers available to reputable firms who may have a product or service of interest to you. If you would prefer we not share your name and address, please check here. ☐

LIREG07

When four little
noisemakers moved in
next door to Wade Dalton,
he didn't expect he'd fall
for the kids and their
beautiful aunt. With Cassie
being at least a dozen
years his junior and Wade
having a secret that would
only make life harder for
them, he had to keep his
distance, but that was
something those four little
blessings weren't about
to let him do!

Look for

Four Little Blessings

by

Merrillee Whren

Available February
wherever books are sold.

Steeple
Hill®

Love Inspired®

TITLES AVAILABLE NEXT MONTH

Don't miss these four stories in February

A DREAM TO SHARE by Irene Hannon
Heartland Homecoming

Mark Campbell was in Missouri to convince Abby Warner to sell
her family's newspaper to his conglomerate. He didn't want to
spend any more time in the one-stoplight town than he had to.
But the feisty newswoman brought out feelings in Mark that were
front-page worthy.

HEALING TIDES by Lois Richer
Pennies from Heaven

Doctors aren't supposed to get attached to patients, yet
GloryAnn Cranbrook couldn't help falling for one sick little boy.
He needed a procedure only her boss, Dr. Jared Steele, could
perform. So why wouldn't he do it? It was up to GloryAnn to
change his mind—and his heart.

FOUR LITTLE BLESSINGS by Merrillee Whren

The four little noisemakers who'd moved next door to
Wade Dalton came with a bonus: their beautiful aunt. Wade
was attracted to the chaos that surrounded them, though he
had a secret that could keep them all apart. Something the four
little blessings weren't about to let happen.

HER UNLIKELY FAMILY by Missy Tippens

Her calling was to help teenage runaways. But when the handsome,
uptight uncle of her newest girl showed up, Josie Miller knew she
was in over her head. Michael Throckmorton didn't know the first
thing about parenting. Maybe she could help them all become a
family.